MERJELLA

MERJELLA

YUVARAJA DHAYANITHI

PARTRIDGE
A Penguin Random House Company

To order additional copies of this book, contact
Partridge India
000 800 10062 62
orders.india@partridgepublishing.com

www.partridgepublishing.com/india

Gift Me

I shall do wonders to your loved ones!

I have the immense pleasure in gifting this book, *Merjella*, authored by Yuvaraja Dhayanithi, to my dear _____ for the occasion _____.

Message:

Date: Signature:

CONTENTS

1   Journey to Zypher.................................13
2   The Funnel of God 17
3   Zypher...23
4   A Long Wait 32
5   Merjella..39
6   Merjella to the Land............................47
7   Ryan's Garage.....................................53
8   Rosy Parker 61
9   Qwerty and the Ring 66
10   Mayor's Party 72
11   Deimos Betrayed.................................78
12   Fabricator at Work 89
13   Terror Strike.......................................96
14   Training Fishes 104
15   Seasorg...110
16   Marina and Deimos 120
17   Mimico Killed...................................126
18   The Boss 133
19   Final Fight at Seasquare....................141
20   Eyecandy Attacked 148
21   Days of Love.....................................155
22   Breaking into Eyecandy.....................164
23   Merjella versus the Boss 170

My sincere thanks to all the souls that
smile on seeing this book!

PREFACE

The story was created under various circumstances. This is my debut novel, and it took me years to complete this work. All those years, lots of things changed. The names changed, the characters changed, the plot changed, but the focus of the story remained the same. The focus is to help today's kids and teens to evolve their thought processes above certain constraints, so they could bud into wonderful creationists and great inventors, who will carry human lives into further sophistication and glory.

As a small step forward, I suggest that you write short stories or even ideas using the characters from this novel and send your creations to us. We shall publish them as separate volumes and spread them to the world. Kindly send your photograph and biodata along with your ideas or stories to merjella@gmail.com.

Follow us on www.facebook.com/merjellathebook

Let's think beyond what is thinkable!

With love,
Yuvaraja Dhayanithi

1

JOURNEY TO ZYPHER

'Do you have to fight, Mimico?'
'What if you lose? What would happen to us? Where would we go?'

'You said they are evil and dishonest. If it's not a fair fight, can you still beat them?'

The wise old Mimico was bombarded with all those questions by his little companions.

The little ones included Jella, a dark-brownish and not-so-appealing octopus. She was very composed and slow-moving. Being brought up under the watchful eyes of Mimico, she was allowed to mingle with very few. Qwerty and Bingo were her only friends in that vast sea. For them, Jella was their only friend, and that made them a family.

The small Qwerty was a bright-yellow fish with a vibrant long purple tail and long ribbon-like fins. She was orphaned as a result of an ongoing family feud with the orange-tailed species. She was bubbly and tended to be garrulous, constantly disturbing Jella with her silly talks and frequent pecks.

Bingo, the glowing green starfish, had fled his home at a very young age in order to avoid the uninspiring daily chores and pressures to bring home his share of food. He was a deep thinker, keen observer, and known to apply logic to all his actions. However, it was always difficult for his friends to get him to talk. Unfortunately, when he chose to unzip his mouth, they always found it far more difficult to have shut him up.

Mimico was a brown-and-white-striped octopus with the ability to imitate other sea creatures. Through their long journey, he had impersonated a lionfish to avoid being spotted by his predators and also by the dangerous Zyphereans.

On that cold, dark night, Mimico was performing his self-assigned duty of guiding the little ones to Zypher.

'You always taught us to avoid fighting at all costs, but now you are taking us miles simply to fight the powerful malojels!' Bingo posed the question to Mimico.

The ever-effervescent Qwerty smirked as she knew it would be tough for Mimico to keep calm after Bingo had opened up.

'Zypher, as we all are aware of, is not a dark empire,' claimed Mimico in a steady voice.

For a moment, Qwerty stood silently as she thought Mimico was going to reveal something important. She silenced herself and showed a certain amount of character by following Mimico's speech.

'Zypher was conceived as a vision—a vision to protect all! A vision to empower all! A vision to enlightenment! A vision that was expected to put a smile to all faces! A vision to bring prosperity and integrity! A vision which not even someone with the wildest of imaginations could claim has any limitations! A vision that could only be rightly called an empire!'

Jella moved close to Mimico so she could listen to him better. Qwerty, on the other hand, felt that Mimico's brief utterance were only his rumblings, and she had already moved a few feet ahead of the group. She then turned back to look at her companions. Her ever-wandering mind was looking for an aperture to amusement. She quickly swam back to join the group.

She then kissed Jella a couple of times and beamed at her. Qwerty's act not only disturbed Mimico's flow of words but also managed to nettle Jella. Jella pushed Qwerty aside and moved closer to Mimico. Not giving up, the playful Qwerty pushed Jella back violently. In the process, Jella hit the nearby rock, and her skin got bruised. Her facetious act invited fury from Mimico.

'Leave her alone, Qwerty!' boomed Mimico rather sternly. This surprised everyone as Mimico was otherwise known to be very much avuncular to Jella's only friends—Bingo and Qwerty.

Mimico's outburst led to a deafening silence. Everyone in the little company knew in their heart of hearts that the journey could not be pursued if Mimico continued to be bad-tempered. They also knew that something would dispel the heavy atmosphere sooner or later.

The sea at night was very vibrant. Though they were travelling at the deepest layer of the photic zone, it was almost totally dark as it was a day before the new-moon day. They enjoyed the sight of those few creatures that lit themselves beautifully in that darkness.

Qwerty was held spellbound as she gazed upon a bluish-green sea anemone. Its beauty seemed to call out to her. With a toss of her head, she raced towards the flower-like creature. She was joined by a playful little lanternfish in her strange pursuit. Just as she was about to enter the hollow white central region of the sea anemone, racing ahead of the lanternfish, she found herself being rudely pulled aside. As she turned angrily to look at her attacker, she saw Mimico watching something else. She turned back to follow his line of vision and saw the beautiful sea anemone having a meal of the hapless lanternfish.

A chill ran down her spine, and she shuddered. Mimico had just saved her from falling prey to the carnivorous plant.

'The world outside is always full of surprises—good as well as bad!'

'I just saw it, Mimico,' Qwerty replied acidly.

'Expressing anger is an art, Qwerty. The more grace you apply to it, the more effective it shall be,' insisted Mimico.

'I am not angry, Mimico. I feel so lost,' said Qwerty as tears welled in her eyes. 'One moment, all my friends love me and want me around, and the next moment, the same buddies appear to hate me.' As she was saying that, her tear gates broke open, and tears flooded the sea.

'Nobody hates you here!' intruded Jella.

'Nobody likes me!' Qwerty started whimpering, and the little group gathered around her in order to calm her down. Soon Qwerty was back to her usual self, and the group continued with their journey.

As they were nearing Zypher, Mimico spied the first streaks of sunlight filtering through the dark-blue water. A new day was being ushered. As he looked up, he sighted a few diurnals. He also saw stern-looking tiger fish patrolling at a distance. Mimico and his little buddies decided that it was time for them to settle in a hideout.

They found a hole between the rocks on the sea floor with a few fissures. The gruelling journey had tired out the little ones, and they soon settled into a deep slumber while Mimico stayed awake to guard his loved ones.

2

THE FUNNEL OF GOD

The little group was rudely jolted out of their sleep by a sudden smacking noise. But their fatigue made them ignore the sound, and they continued to sleep. Within a few seconds, there was a pleasant fragrance filling the water there. They could not resist their curiosity further, and they peeped out cautiously to investigate. Their eyes beheld a strange and wondrous sight. They saw a machine that seemed to be producing the whizzing sound. But what was stranger was the sight that followed. Several groups of fishes, old and young, rushed towards the machine with inexplicable urgency.

The machine, with a wide funnel-shaped opening at the bottom, rested there with three adjustable legs like a tripod to balance and enable the whole machine to stand straight. There was just enough space for little shoals of fishes to gather underneath. The giant machine started sucking up the fishes in bunches, and yet the whole place appeared to have an atmosphere akin to a place of worship.

While they were watching from behind the hole, a young and rather handsome fish caught their attention. His face radiated an expression of utter peace and joy as he waited for his turn to enter the lane between the tripod legs of the machine.

'Dear son, God will definitely accept you! Offer your prayers sincerely!' His proud father beamed from a distance. As he turned back to look, the father waved his only fin. His left fin was missing.

'Goodbye, Daddy! I have never sinned. At God's court, I will plead for you! I shall always make you proud, Dad!' The son waved back his fins and moved towards the funnel-shaped machine and was absorbed.

'I should have listened to my daddy. He insisted me not to stray with my friends, but I never listened. I couldn't save myself unscathed when the shark attacked us that night, and this broken fin invited anger from God. That's why he rejected me,' recalled the father for the thousandth time, talking to his wife.

'We have raised our son disciplined, and he will make us proud, dear,' consoled the mother even as tears welled in her eyes.

'What is that, Mimico?' asked the awestruck Jella, pointing towards the giant funnel-shaped object.

'Well, it is called the funnel of God! It is the way the Almighty takes back the lives of those fishes that are pure of heart and untouched by sin. It is believed that the good Lord summons them and allows them the privilege of living in his kingdom, where there is only peace, love, and joy.'

It was then that they heard a sound that seemed like distant wailing. A few fishes were sobbing plaintively as they fell back into the water from the funnel of God.

'How have I sinned, Mummy? Why did God reject me?' questioned a crestfallen little fish as she continued to weep. Her mother looked helpless as she tried to console the little fish.

'In the distant past, it is said that God simply dropped a small string which bore a hook. All fishes would fight to get to the hook. Only a few ever managed to get to the hook, but those who did never returned. God accepted everyone in those days. The old-timers say it was quite painful to undertake a journey through God's hook. But as the old adage goes, "No pain, no gain",' reflected Mimico.

'Do you know why God rejected her, Mimico?' asked Bingo.

'Going by the features of the folks that have been sent back, it can be assumed that in order to enter the kingdom of God, one needs to stay in shape and protect one's body against any injury or disease. In short, God accepts those who have sincerely sheltered their body and soul as presented by him.'

'Have you ever tried to get to God?' Jella asked her mentor.

'Do you believe in God?' This one was from Qwerty.

'Well, to me, it is not all about the existence of God! I believe or don't believe, but I do respect others' sentiments.'

'You never have a *yes* or *no* answer for a *yes* or *no* question, do you?' quizzed Bingo.

'A simple question need not have a simple answer, Bingo! And in the case of the existence of God, let me explain it to you this way. Assume that I am your boss, that you are all working for me, and that you are all being assigned some work to do. Bingo is the kind who is focused and keeps up with his task despite whatever is happening around. He doesn't even care to see me before he completes his assignment. Jella is the one who comes to me often, asking for clarifications about work and bringing to my notice her misfortunes at home and thanking me for all I have done and also sharing everything she got. And Qwerty is the kind who will always praise me and accompany me and try to pass information on to me from others and do nothing else. Now tell me who should be my favourite: Bingo, for sincerely sticking to the job being assigned; or Jella, for sharing all good and bad in her life; or Qwerty, for always accompanying me and praising me at large?'

'Very tricky,' replied Bingo.

'Yes, tricky, of course! If I am after fame, I would enjoy Qwerty's company. If I am after emotions, I would enjoy Jella's company. If I am after nothing and I am everything, I would definitely appreciate Bingo's way.'

'Very true, Mimico!'

'Now, the same applies to God. The priests and other holy fishes are just like Qwerty. They only please the Lord, but fail to accomplish what they are sent for. The ones who offer prayers at will and show themselves at every opportunity to either complain about their wretched life or to thank him are like Jella. They haven't got the right groove over life and lack focus. God will only be tired of those. But Bingo is kind the Almighty will always be proud of.'

'That's a nice thought, Mimico! If there is no god, the prayers are useless, and if there is god, they become senseless!'

'Perfect, Bingo! That's right, isn't it?'

'Agnosticism, right!' confirmed Jella.

'Nah! Damnosticism!' said Bingo wittingly.

Everyone had a hearty laugh.

'Well, yes, damnosticism. I don't give a damn whether he exists or not. I have my duties, and I go with that,' affirmed Mimico.

'Mimico! You haven't yet told us why you have to go for the fight,' asked Bingo.

Mimico observed silence for a few seconds while the kids were looking up at him.

'I am about to disclose a secret to you,' said Mimico.

The little ones looked closer at him to catch his next line.

'Jella is not an ordinary octopus,' declared Mimico.

Even as the curiosity among the juniors, including Jella, rose, Mimico maintained calmness.

'What makes her special?' questioned Bingo, unable to bear the silence.

'Because she is a jellopus.'

'Jellopus!' the little ones reverberated out of excitement.

'No, she cannot be! Jellopuses are mythological characters—like angels. They never existed. Moreover, Jella doesn't look like a jellopus.' Qwerty refused to believe it.

'What do you know about jellopuses?' quizzed Mimico to the challengers.

'Mmmm . . . they are angels! I mean, they look like angels—beautiful! Like . . . colourful, glassy, jelly-like bodies . . . so perfect!' stated Bingo very thoughtfully.

Even as he was saying this, the rest of the company was staring at him. He realized his blunder and started chewing his words.

'Well . . . yes, Jella is beautiful. She looks like an angel. In fact, she acts like an angel. But she is not an angel . . . like a real angel!' Bingo explained his stand.

'Jellopuses are powerful. They can do anything.' Qwerty came to his support. They both nodded, looking at each other, confirming their own knowledge about the jellopuses.

'And Jella is no exception. She is beautiful, and she is indeed powerful. She can travel between time spaces and transform any life to anything,' Mimico enlightened the youngsters.

The three looked at him in disbelief, and Mimico added, 'And Jella is the rightful ruler of Zypher.'

'Only the malojels can rule Zypher,' protested Bingo.

'You are wrong, Bingo. Zypher was created and ruled by jellopuses. Malojels cunningly entered the kingdom and took over. They abandoned all accords with the jellopuses and took advantage of the jellopuses' generosity and honesty to destroy them.'

'But jellopuses are very powerful, right?' Bingo still had his doubts.

'Yes, they are. Jellopuses and malojels are the two powerful species among octopuses and jellyfish. They can transform any life into any other and into any shape and into any dimension. They can go invisible themselves and also make others vanish. They can extend their lifespan by two ways: saving lives and destroying lives. Jellopuses chose their way to immortality through saving lives while the crooked malojels took the path of destroying lives. That made jellopuses even more powerful. They can travel to anywhere and to any time—past, present, or future—at their will, which malojels cannot do. Jellopuses can bring back a lost life. The only thing a jellopus can't do is to recover themselves or another jellopus or any other octopus from death.'

'Then how did we lose the kingdom to them?'

'That's a long story, Jella. But we do have all the time in the world to look back.'

3

ZYPHER

'Zypher was created as a vast empire, a society built to accommodate all kinds of beings and facilitate harmony and prosperity. It was an open-to-all kingdom, a kingdom created to celebrate brotherhood among fishes and a place that would say no to nobody! A dreamland!' Mimico looked so ecstatic and honoured to just utter the word *Zypher*. He continued with his narration.

Even before the jellopuses started actualizing the dream of Zypher, conflicts were ignited by the malojels. They never liked fishes from different communities coming together for a cause—a cause that remained abstruse to many.

The malcontents were waiting for Zypher to go all messy, but that was not to happen. Under the able leadership of Tarjo, Zypher started sparkling like a diamond in the sea. The openness of Zypher invited constant attacks from the jealous malojels, who had no ideals to back their deeds. Later on, when they were confronted, they discovered terms like *power-sharing*, *participation*, *voice of commons*, and whatnots.

Tarjo's period witnessed the advent of the era of science and technology. Several discoveries and inventions triggered revolution that made the lives of the fishes easy and adorable.

Artificial sails and fins were designed to help transport the old and the physically challenged. Sea carts were made out of shells and were widely used to transport goods.

Oil spills were discovered, and refining techniques were developed to extract oil and use them as fuel for various purposes. Later, as an alternative source for oil, they invented ways to extract it from the dead fishes by effectively organizing body donation schemes.

The properties of various planktons and zooplanktons were uncovered and learnt for them to be used in the art of healing incurable diseases.

Expeditions were sponsored and climbing rocks above sea level was promoted by offering big rewards.

During his tenure, it was discovered that there were several water bodies in this world, and there was even high speculation that there may be fish elsewhere too but in different forms.

Agriculture was promoted, and modern technologies were introduced for the purpose of increasing productivity. Genes were discovered, and hybrids were created.

Artists were encouraged, and several carnivals were organized. Various new musical instruments were designed and promoted for the entertainment of fish folk. Schools were incepted, and knowledge was imparted with no discrimination. Living was made easier and blissful, as also the lifespan of the fishes improved noticeably.

In a short time, Tarjo gained popularity. The fishes soon got acculturated to Zypher, and everyone started labouring for the prosperity of Zypher. That only embittered the malojels, and they kept drawing blood from the innocent citizens. Suicide bombing and terror attacks were the order of the day then.

'Bombing!' exclaimed Qwerty.

'Yes, the bombs were created by jellopuses for the purpose of chasing away dangerous predators, like sharks and whales. Malojels first stole them but later started developing them on their own. They wanted to create chaos and wanted everyone to lose belief in Zypher. It was then that Emperor Tarjo called on the rebels for peace talks. The kind man offered to share power with malojels on alternating years—the following year to be ruled by malojels and the next by jellopuses and likewise.'

But the cantankerous Chiro, the leader of the malojels was not quite happy with the offer. He insisted that the next year has twelve new moons while the following year has thirteen, so that would mean an extra new-moon day for the jellopuses to be in power.

'What difference can one day make, Chiro?' Tarjo remarked with his witty accent, and the assembly broke out in laughter in unison even as Chiro cringed. Yet Tarjo was willing to heed Chiro's demands, which were way too ambitious. Chiro demanded two continuous years of power starting next year.

'In that case, we will allot the year after next year to you, Chiro!' said the big-hearted Tarjo.

'That is not fair, Tarjo. Unacceptable.'

'What is the problem with that, Chiro? You will have one extra new-moon day of power!' Tarjo said with the same witty accent. The assembly again broke out in laughter.

'We will have to wait long for that, Tarjo. Moreover, you will be enjoying power for too long a period,' Chiro said after the laughter had subsided in the court.

The assembly felt it was indeed a complex problem for Tarjo to handle, and most of the members showed annoyance at the tight-fisted Chiro.

'Okay then! The next year of rule is for you, and the following year for us. If that one additional new-moon day bothers you very much, then we will host a grand party for the malojels at the Royal Den in the middle of the year in our next tenure. The sharing of power applies to all departments except the law and order enforcement, judiciary, and defence departments, which will be handled by jellopuses only,' declared Tarjo.

'Why should we accept this pact that doesn't entitle us to any power, Tarjo? Do we look like some shameless creatures living to eat delicious food thrown at us by you? Malojels are no beggars, Tarjo!' bawled the angry Chiro.

Dofleini, one of Tarjo's elderly ministers, intruded. 'If our king saw you as beggars, you wouldn't be here with equal respect to him. What would you settle for, Chiro?'

'I need that day to be special. I want absolute power on that one day and for us to be treated as guests.'

Without dragging the issue any further, Tarjo heeded to his demands and declared that, apart from the royal feast, the malojels would have absolute power on the seventh new-moon day of the year after next year.

As agreed, Chiro acceded to the throne on New Year's Day, and the celebrations were sky-high. Chiro in power was clearly visible, with the maladroit administration and faltering developments. However, Tarjo's folks managed to keep the system in balance by imposing effective control over the crucial departments. Though Chiro's hands were tied, he made best abuse of his powers to mangle the system by appointing his loyalists to all possible state vacancies. He even diverted funds illegally to develop a private army, the Chironers, outside Zypher.

After a long year, Tarjo took over again and was left with lots of reforms to be done. Legal and administrative changes were brought about to tighten the loopholes in the system. Despite threats from Chiro and his supporters, Tarjo kept pressing his revamping activities. Tarjo's team raided all the Chironers' camps and took them as prisoners. Most of the Chironers were notorious tiger fish and swordfish that were trained to attack ruthlessly. All those flouting the law were taught their deserved lessons. The mood in Chiro's camp became gloomy and vengeful. The poisons were waiting for a day—a convenient day— to run through the veins of Tarjo's territory.

The day approached. The day of absolute power for the malojels was at sight, and Tarjo took all precautionary measures for that day. Additional securities were installed; unwarranted transits were stalled. Treasured loyalists were backed up; treacherous counterparts were packed up.

The borders of Zypher were sealed and installed with more security measures. Despite Tarjo's councillors advising him to have the palace secured, Tarjo insisted on sending palace guards to the border. He was aware Chiro would release the prisoners with his powers and that they would escape. So he wanted his best squad at a distance; the escaping convicts would reach in a days' time. He knew well that the malojels would not dare to attack them as they have always experienced the might of jellopuses.

Tarjo's wife, Velodona, was lying weak with her newly born babies. She was weak as she had neglected to feed herself for weeks while the eggs were hatching. Her health did not recover even when the best of medical treatments were provided. She finally died on the eve of the new-moon day.

The group of ministers who were beside Tarjo on that dreadful moment decided to cancel the new-moon day celebration. But Tarjo did not want to stop the proceedings.

'We have given our word. It is not just a celebration, but a night of hope for the malojels. We should not deny them that,' Tarjo told them.

After the ministers and well-wishers had dispersed slowly, Mimico was the last man standing with Emperor Tarjo. Mimico was his faithful intelligence chief, who ran the spy network very efficiently for Tarjo.

'Chiro is planning to attack us tomorrow, milord,' Mimico informed Tarjo, who was looking at his thousand newborn babies. He picked up with his two arms a tender baby, whose eyes were yet to see the light.

'Hold her, Mimico.' Tarjo passed her to Mimico's arms. 'She is the chosen one, Mimico.'

Young Mimico looked up to see the eyes of Tarjo.

'I foresee something terrible for tomorrow, Mimico. The baby you are holding is the one who is going to save the world. Remember, she is the chosen one, Mimico. In twenty moons, she will turn into a powerful jellopus and destroy evil of every form,' said Tarjo.

'But why not stop tomorrow's madness and save the world today?' Mimico questioned.

'No, Mimico. She is the one destined to save the world. And the world doesn't end with what we know of today,' stressed Tarjo, and he ordered Mimico to leave Zypher.

When Mimico took a deep look at the eyes of Tarjo, the emperor instructed, 'Name her Jella.'

Mimico left Zypher with Jella wrapped in his arms.

As midnight approached, malojels and octopuses started to arrive at the Royal Den. At the stroke of midnight, the party kicked off with colourful events performed by octopuses. New-moon nights were always special among octopuses and jellyfish as they can showcase their skills with colour and luminescence in that utter darkness.

On the backstage, as expected, Chiro ordered the release of Chironers, but the expected thing did not happen. The freed Chironers did not flee after being released but instead surrounded the palace. The regular guards were made to disown their weapons and were issued marching orders.

Tarjo received warning signals soon, and there prevailed tension in the room, with Chiro and Tarjo glaring at each other's eyes. Who would blink first?

When the jellyfish had to perform their ethnic arts, Chiro took the stage to exhibit his talents. Imitating a magician, Chiro pulled out a wentletrap shell with yellow pigments and let it dissolve in the water. The water inside the den turned pale yellow, and the armed Chironers stormed in. They blocked all the passages leading to and exiting the Royal Den and started slaying the jellopuses with no mercy. The sharp swords were wielded at random to milk the blood of the royal jellopuses. The efforts of jellopuses to go invisible went vain as the yellow pigment highlighted their whereabouts.

With four of the malojels clutching Tarjo's arms with their strong tentacles, Chiro strutted towards him with vengeful eyes.

'What difference can one day make, Chiro?' Chiro mimicked Tarjo's witty accent. 'Can you see now what difference one day can make, Tarjo?' uttered Chiro in his crude voice.

Chiro then got hold of Tarjo tightly and gave a sucker punch with his venomous arm, saying, 'It takes just one second for my arm to sting and spit poison through your body.'

Tarjo could have ejected ink from his sac and made Chiro numb for the rest of his life. But he did not wish to make any offensive move on that day as he saw malojels as his guests.

Chiro took advantage of this and said, 'It takes just one second to disgrace a dynamic leader.' He rubbed Tarjo's wounded part with a murex shell, and as Tarjo felt the immense pain, Chiro said, 'It takes just one second to condemn an emperor to deep pain.'

Chiro then signalled the fellow malojels to loosen their grip on the dying emperor. As Tarjo fell downwards, Chiro, with his face blooming with malicious pleasure, continued saying, 'It takes just one second to ground a prince. It takes just a few seconds to destroy one's dreams. It takes just a few seconds to wipe out a community. It takes just a few seconds to slip from hero to zero. And a day consists of thousands of such seconds to do all these.' He again imitated Tarjo's words, '"What difference can one day make, Chiro?" Huh!'

Tarjo calmly replied back, 'All that you said was about destruction, Chiro. But it takes pride to create, not to destroy!'

The enraged Chiro stamped Tarjo's body with another sting, saying, 'This very second, you may rest!'

As Tarjo hit the bottom of the floor, he was still alive. Chiro went near him to have a closer look.

'The mechanical heart that pumps blood has stopped. The emotional heart that beats out of love has stopped. But there is a third heart that carries the hopes of a million lives and it refuses to stop. You may have to use all your venom to bring it to a halt, Chiro' hinted Tarjo.

Chiro, with all his might and a ton of arms, stung Tarjo one last time to inject all his venom simultaneously. Tarjo finally died.

By that time, the Chironers successfully got rid of other jellopuses too. All the octopuses were captured, and later they were imprisoned.

4

A LONG WAIT

When Mimico finished narrating the history of Zypher, Jella was lying embraced by one of his arms.

'Am I a jellopus?' asked Jella.

'Yes, you are, Jella.'

'What about my siblings? Why didn't my dad choose any of them?'

'Not all the octopuses are jellopuses. Only one in few thousands grows into a jellopus. And nobody knows who will become one. It takes a few moons to become a jellopus, and they become more and more powerful with more and more lives they save,' explained Mimico.

Jella looked sad. She looked at Mimico and said, 'I am not going to become a jellopus. Twenty moons are over. I don't see any such sign, Mimico. I have failed my dad.'

'Don't be so dejected, Jella. You will live to save this world for sure. Tarjo's words have never gone wrong,' consoled Mimico.

'Can we not just raise an army and defeat the malojels?' posed Jella.

'No, Jella. It is not possible. The fishes we live with are all civilians. They cannot fight like octopuses or jellyfish do. Unfortunately, jellopuses have all been destroyed, and octopuses are all imprisoned.'

'What about the sharks and whales, Mimico? They have more strength, right?' asked Qwerty.

'They are only predators, Qwerty. They can't think beyond killing and feeding. They cannot be motivated to fight. They are not just good for fighting. You don't take killers for warfare. We only need the ones with killer instincts to fight.'

'I thought killer instinct is synonymous with killers.'

'No, Qwerty. They are not. A killer only knows to kill for reasons known only to him. The killer instinct is the quality one exhibits naturally with a strong urge to win but not kill.'

'Killing one's enemy is the sweetest way of winning, right?' Bingo interrupted.

'You are not right, Bingo. The best form of victory is demoralizing and taking full control of one's enemy, forcing him to concede defeat, and having him live with his pride dented.'

'What do you plan to do, Mimico?' asked Bingo.

'Chiro celebrates every new-moon day as the National Day of Zypher. Apart from colourful activities, they organize fights too to display their supremacy. Chiro has announced the release of political prisoners if any octopus can wrestle to win Nomura.'

'Nomura!' exclaimed Jella.

'Yes, Nomura—his aide!'

'Don't you see that it is a trap to capture the remaining free-living octopuses?'

'Yes, it is. But I have information to believe that the challenge is genuine and will be fairly played. Moreover, it is a public event, and Chiro may want to look generous.'

'So you have informers from Zypher?'

'Yes, my expertise is in espionage, Qwerty. I always have a very good network.'

'But still . . .' Bingo dragged with his words.

'Winning doesn't come free of risk, Bingo. But we are not going to risk everything. It will be only me going to the ring while you will be coming to the Seasquare to watch the fight. Jella and Qwerty will remain here till either you or both of us return.'

'What if something happens to you?' Jella asked.

'I will be jailed, Jella. But you will get stronger soon. You can rescue every one of us.'

'But then you can wait till then, Mimico. Why go now? There is no point,' observed Bingo.

'True. But I see a win-win situation for us here. If I manage to beat Nomura, I will get the octopuses released right away. Even if I don't win, I will be getting the chance to interact with the long-imprisoned octopuses and work out strategies. It will get easier when you put up the last fight. My work with you for now is over, Jella. I need to give other octopuses hope and help with their morale.'

'But then, I may not be a jellopus,' said Jella.

'You are a jellopus. Believe in yourself, Jella. My job was to raise you safely for twenty moons, and it is done with. Now it is my duty to feed energy into my swarm.'

Mimico did not entertain more questions from the little mates.

They then started to hunt for food. Zooplanktons were their chief food. Every time they dined, they made a habit of teasing the way Qwerty nibbled her food. The rest of the company usually gobbled the food and sometimes left very little for Qwerty.

After the meal, Mimico wanted to rest for a while before going to Seasquare. He also insisted for Bingo to have some rest. Though they rested, no one did really sleep.

As day turned to dusk, Mimico and Bingo got ready and left for Zypher. Mimico did not forget to leave special instructions to both Qwerty and Jella.

'Jella, remember that whatever situation you are in, you should always do good and save lives. Bingo, Qwerty, you should stay by her side. Always keep in mind, she is very special.' Mimico then hugged Jella and kissed her goodbye.

Jella and Qwerty started off what was going to become a very long wait. Time stood like the water in the deep sea. After a few minutes, both Jella and Qwerty got restless. They were constantly thinking about what was going to happen to Mimico.

'What does the Seasquare look like?' asked Qwerty.

'It is a big square rock over which the challengers wrestle each other.'

'How do you know that?'

'Mimico used to tell me about Seasquare and the rules followed. But he never told me about Zypher.'

'Do we need to kill the opponent to win the fight?'

'No, Qwerty! We just need to take control of our opponent, and the end of the fight will be decided by the referee, who will tap the rock to the count of three. The loser will then be declared as a slave to the winner, and he cannot challenge him for another year.'

'Do you know what Nomoral looks like?'

The puzzled Jella quizzed back, 'Nomoral?'

'Yes, right, Nomoral. That's how I would've named him.'

'Huh! You would name Nomura as *Nomoral*.' Jella laughed out loud.

'Why not? *Nomoral* should suit him well!' declared Qwerty.

Jella continued to laugh her head off.

'Stop laughing like that, Jella. A name should suit one's personality, making it easy to associate with.'

'Like?'

'Like, whatever name that doesn't sound or fit one's character doesn't make sense. Don't you think a name is like a soul to go together with a being?'

'Well, yeah, right! Er . . . mmm . . . What do you think of my name?'

'It fits you very much, you know! It goes well! I mean, it gels with you! It's a name that tells you are an angel and that you gel well with friends. Like a jelly.'

'What about Mimico?'

'Perfect name for his mimicking nature and his motherly commitments. What do you say?'

'Yes, yes! And Bingo?'

'Frankly, it should be the worst-suited name for him. B-I-N-G-O! Ha ha ha! I would have named him D-U-M-B-O!'

'Oh really? So how would you have named yourself?'

'I don't need to. It fits me so aptly.'

'Oh? Tell me how your name suits you, Miss Qwerty!'

'Maybe it means I am a quick-witted, real thinker, yo!'

'Oh! That means it should be Q-W-R-T-Y—not *Qwerty*, but *Qwrty*! Hmm . . . maybe it means 'quack, whack, eek, ruck, tuck, yuck!' Saying that, Jella punched and tapped Qwerty's rapidly angering cheeks.

Qwerty, out of resentment, started hitting Jella with her fins and tried dashing at her. But Jella managed to arrest her movements with a twist of her arms, and after Qwerty calmed down, she let her go.

For the next few minutes, Qwerty seethed around, gauging the size of the hideout and traversing every nook of that boring place. Jella was quietly watching Qwerty's angry moments and paltry movements.

Soon Qwerty found a way to amuse herself by starting to collect the flowers and colourful pebbles available in the vicinity. At first, Qwerty was very choosy, carefully watching out for flaws, but later on, she started to pick everything that caught her attention. She collected them all on a flat oval black rock.

As the time slowly passed by, Jella too started to feel the heat. For the first time, Jella started showing some anxious movements. She moved to the hind side of a cave-shaped structure and peeped at the distance to see if she could find any pleasurable sight, but she was deeply disappointed.

Though Qwerty was eagerly looking at her face for reactions, she turned away when Jella looked at her. It was quite evident her anger had not yet diluted enough to bring out the playful kid in her. Jella still enjoyed the sight of watching Qwerty in such a committed mode of acquiring the collectibles.

Qwerty did not seem to mind anything happening around. With the help of a slender long twig, she started to fix and arrange the flowers together. Jella could not stay away for long from the silent Qwerty. She rumpled the flowers organized by Qwerty.

'Don't be such a meanie!' shouted Qwerty at Jella.

'Oh, meanie! You mean to say I should be named Jelly Meanie?'

'Exactly! Meanie Jelly!' reiterated Qwerty with a sharp stare at her.

'Oh, oh! So what are you trying to do by deglamourizing these beautiful flowers and ferns?'

'A bouquet!'

'A bouquet?'

'Yes, a bouquet for our triumphant team!'

'Well! In that case, I will offer my hands too.' After saying that, Jella joined Qwerty in making a beautiful bouquet.

Jella and Qwerty attempted to showcase their artistic skills, trying to outclass each other. Jella was using red as the theme colour while Qwerty was using her favourite, blue. They were so involved in the work that they minded little about the time flashing by.

Too soon, their newfound hobby saturated their creative instincts, and the anxiety running deep down their nerves started to bulge out. In that dark night, not even the moon chose to accompany them. The sea and their hopes got darker as time passed by. Then the disheartened friends fell asleep unawares.

5

MERJELLA

Jella and Qwerty were sleeping when Bingo arrived around midnight. He hurriedly woke them up. Since they were sleeping after a tiring journey and a very long wait, they found it hard to get up. But when they realized that Bingo had returned alone, their sleepiness evaporated. Without saying anything, Bingo rushed them to leave the place. Jella and Qwerty did not forget to take the bouquet and the garland, which they plucked and dispersed on their way back.

It was a dreary journey as Bingo chose to keep silent while Jella and Qwerty were scared to learn the truth. They plodded on with heavy hearts. As their hunger had not been taken care of, it grew alarming.

Unlike the onward journey, they moved in pace. Qwerty did not speed up—not because she was tired and hungry, but because the need she felt to stay close to her friends in that disastrous time kept her to stay abreast. What was more surprising was the way Qwerty kept herself silent.

Finally, there was something to dissipate the frozen air.

'What happened to Mimico?' asked Qwerty amidst that stillness.

Jella shot an eager look at Bingo, who chose not to open up but move ahead silently. They continued the journey in a glum fashion, guided by very mildly illuminated sea creatures.

'They played foul.' The words tumbled out from Bingo's mouth. Bingo could not hold his emotions any longer.

'What happened to Mimico?' asked Jella.

'He was taken as prisoner too. Before he took the square, he told me he won't be making it. But he asks you to be positive and to live with no fear. He also wants you to help others at any cost, and that trait will bring you glory.'

'He always tells me that,' recalled Jella.

Soon it started to dawn, and they were far away from Zypher.

Suddenly, they heard a huge thud, accompanied by a mild tremor in the area. They turned to see the cause, and it was the funnel of God, which had stalled there. A sensor zoomed out, with a laser beam scanning the area. By that time, a large number of fishes had gathered and were jostling to take the divine plunge.

A few elderly fishes were staying back, and in chorus, they started to recite slogans in appreciation of God.

> God! God! Dear God!
> Take us, we're pure by heart!
> God! God! Dear God!
> Give us your divine nod!

While Jella and Bingo watched the mad melee, something that they could hardly believe happened. Qwerty fell prey to the rituals with her irrational move to reach God. Everything happened in a flash that both Jella and Bingo were shell-shocked. They were so confused whether to pray to God to send her back or to take her with him. If Qwerty was to return, then she would live the rest of her life in despair.

They stood there for some time to see if she was coming back, being rejected by God. As fishes were expelled batch by batch, they earnestly looked to identify their friend. As the funnel of God was finally disengaged, the place resembled a funeral ground, with cries and howls getting louder as there were a few left dead. With no sign of Qwerty being sent back, the depressed Jella and Bingo moved ahead quietly.

'God is sometimes cruel. There is nothing wrong with malojels considering him evil,' said Bingo.

'Don't talk stupid. God is always good,' insisted Jella to Bingo.

There was a brief silence, and then Jella questioned, 'What did he look like?'

'Who?'

'Nomura!'

'Meh, he looked so awful. He is just big. Mmm . . . very big, huge, humongous! Smelled dreadful! Short arms. He is not very strong. His movements were slow but tactful. Uh . . . deceptive moves. But not totally invincible!'

'Poor Mimico! He is too old. We shouldn't have let him go.'

'Mimico is a stronger fighter, Jella. In fact, he pounded Nomura with much ease and forced him to submission.'

'Then what happened?'

'They cheated. They tampered with the rules.'

'We warned him. He didn't listen.'

There was a bit of silence as Jella's questions in her mind dried up.

'We should fight them,' said Bingo.

'I am lost, Bingo. I don't find a reason to live.'

'No, Jella. Actually, you have more reasons to live, Jella—to save Mimico and other octopuses in jail and to capture Zypher and establish a fair and just empire. I saw many octopuses there, Jella. They are all good souls. Many of your siblings are there too. We should save them, Jella.'

Jella understood her importance and nodded positively to Bingo's words. 'Didn't you have any trouble getting out of there?'

'No. The moment we reached there, Mimico introduced me to Aurelia.'

'Aurelia?'

'Yes, Aurelia! She is an angel. She has her own ways of getting things done. She commands huge respect in Zypher. She guided me to an exit once Mimico was captured.'

'Who else did you meet there, Bingo?'

'I saw Joubin. They say she was a famous singer. There were talks that her songs attracted many to Zypher during Tarjo's days. She was singing songs of bravery, encouraging young octopuses to take on Nomura.'

'Did others fight too?'

'Yes, they did, but with only two arms freed. The rest were tied up. Still they managed to put up a brave fight, Jella.'

'What else happened there, Bingo?'

'The octopuses were offered a special feast and were treated as guests. Even then, they had only two arms freed. Malojels are very scared of the octopuses. They will never sleep if they come to know about you, Jella! A jellopus alive will be their worst nightmare!'

Jella was disturbed by that statement, and she kept moving. But all of a sudden, she started to writhe with tremendous pain. She felt uncomfortable and did not know what had gotten into her. She felt that the pain was unbearable, and for a moment, she thought she had lost her guts to brave a simple pain. She felt powerless. She felt the pain all over her body.

Bingo stood helplessly watching Jella shriek out in pain. He saw her skin cracking here and there. The chill of the atmosphere must be inflicting such sharp pain to the parts exposed. Bingo was surprised to see a pinkish glow inside her skin.

'You are a jellopus,' Bingo said in his mind. 'The pink is not your blood. It is your new skin. The glow! No sign of your blue blood. You are a jellopus.' He looked at her, unmoving.

Suddenly, they smelled the odour of blood, but Jella was not bleeding. With a lot of confusion, they looked around, and the sharks were not far away. As they continued with the investigation, they saw a streak of blood from above, which was fast diffusing into the blue sea. They traced the source of blood and saw an alien body struggling for life. They could feel the intensity of her craving to live by the strong vibes created by her decelerating heartbeat.

'What is that, Jella? It looks like some alien,' guessed Bingo doubtfully.

'I too don't know what it is. Some alien creature, it should be.' Jella moved nearer to the alien body. Despite her skin cracking, she remained stoic. Bingo followed her.

The alien creature was indeed a young lady—stabbed and thrown into the sea. There was no movement in her except the pounding of her heart.

'It has four long arms and some fifteen, sixteen, maybe twenty mini arms, but no suction cups,' observed Jella.

Bingo, who was behind her, focused on changes he could see in Jella. Jella's skin continued to peel off, and the luminescence became very visible.

'Aah . . . a beautiful face. Eyes are large . . . black. It could be an angel,' Jella continued with her observation on the lady.

But Bingo was not interested in Jella's findings. Jella had turned completely pink, and her new skin radiated astonishingly. While he kept staring at Jella, he saw a large shark fast approaching.

'Jella! Watch out!' he shouted.

Jella turned back and saw a huge shark charging with all vigour. Jella ejected black ink from her ink sac and kept a firm hold on the lady's hair. The ink cloud confused the olfactory sense of the predator, and the shark stood static for a few seconds. At that time, Jella dragged the lady by her hair as far away as she could from the shark. When the ink cloud cleared, the shark could both see and smell the blood again.

Jella looked around to find a place to hide. She spotted a small tunnel with an opening wide enough to enter. Being devoid of any hard structure in her body, Jella easily squeezed through, but she found it hard to pull the lady into that small hole. Bingo, who had followed them, pushed the lady from outside. Jella put all her suction cups over the lady's body and, with all force, sucked and pulled her inwards. Right when the shark's sharp teeth almost reached to get a bite of the lady, Jella managed to pull her into the tunnel, and along came the starfish with a couple of spins.

When Bingo opened his eyes after balancing himself, he could not believe what he saw. The lady's size diminished when Jella pulled her in, and with that force, she went straight inside Jella's mouth.

Jella's body went through some rapid amoebic transformations. Jella, with the lady inside her, began to deform and reform, taking on random shapes. Bingo was unable to believe what he was witnessing. For Jella, it was so painful that she was shaken vigorously in the water, completely out of control. She then fainted, and she dropped down to the sea floor, on the bed of the beautiful ball-shaped white anemones.

Bingo moved near her and took a close look at her. Jella's face had new features. The lady's face was visible through her radiant body. She looked like a mermaid in disguise of Jella. Bingo slowly shook her, trying to wake her up.

'Why did they kill me?' questioned Jella when she got up, and without looking for any answer, she kept staring at the spectacular underwater creatures.

'Who? You are alive, Jella. You are alive!' Bingo shook her.

'Alive? Yes, I am alive! Who are you?' Jella asked, confused.

'Who am I? Who are you then? What happened to you, Jella?' asked Bingo.

'Who . . . Jella? Who? Me? Marjine . . . Ma . . . Marina Jellancy . . . Jelencia . . . Marjinna . . . Marjella . . . Merjola—'

'Jella! Do you remember me?' Bingo shook her again.

'Bingo, what do you mean by 'Who are you?' Something's happening to me, Bingo.' Suddenly, her tone changed. Jella felt like she was in a familiar zone.

'What? What's happening, Jella? You just swallowed an angel who was five times bigger than you! You have to let that out of you, Jella.'

Jella started to search for something while Bingo was very much puzzled about what was happening. Bingo followed her, trying to help. Her memories as the lady and as Jella were alternating, and she was in a confused state.

'What are you looking for, Jella?'

'Marina. Call me Marina. Where am I?' Jella's voice sounded different. It was sweeter and more gracious.

'Your voice has changed. The angel has got into you, Jella.'

'Yes, Bingo. I could feel that. I am now one body of two lives—Marina and Jella.'

'Merjella?' asked Bingo.

'Yes, I am Merjella!'

6

MERJELLA TO THE LAND

It took some time for Merjella to realize her state. She could run visuals on her mind screen of her being stabbed. Yet her memories as Marina before she was stabbed were not easy to recall. But as Jella, she could remember every detail.

Though she looked a lot different from other lives in the water, she looked very much created for the aquatic life. Her translucent pinkish body with Marina's protruding face was a delight to watch. Her features—which included gorgeous round black eyes with eyelids, mouth with reddish lips, and Marina's hair that was covered with a translucent thick jelly layer—made her look unique. On the back of her face, concealed completely under the jelly hair, were Jella's brownish beak and her original large eyes. The eyes on both sides of her face allowed her to see on all sides.

Deep inside, Merjella felt different. She felt rejuvenated. She was feeling restless, and her arms were itching to do something.

Bingo was very tired and droopy while Merjella's eyes were wide open, watching the deep aquatic life. Though the sight was a usual one for Jella, Marina inside was so ecstatic in seeing the colourful underwater creatures. The splendour of the seabed and the constant activities of fishes kept her eyes engaged.

A purple fish with a long black tail and yellow stripes, who was pushing her way through the scrappy rocks, caught Merjella's attention. The fast fluttering of the wavy yellow-striped tail of the fish was a delightful sight for the kind of patterns it generated. When the fish crossed the rocks, the tail was seen fluttering fast but not waving like before, and so the patterns were missing. Merjella noticed blood seeping from her scratched body.

Merjella felt sorry for that injured fish. She could feel the pain of the fish. She wanted to help her. She tried focusing on the fish. As her focus on the fish intensified, her face gave numerous funny expressions accompanied by a squeaky noise. That disrupted Bingo's sleep and woke him up. He tried to understand what was going on, but he could not get a hint. Suddenly, she erupted with enormous joy and danced with all her arms spread out. It was a delightful sight for Bingo.

'May I know the reason for your amusement?' questioned Bingo.

'I am a jellopus, Bingo. I am a jellopus!' shouted Merjella in joy.

Bingo kept looking at her with no reaction.

'I did it! I just did it, Bingo.'

'What did you do, Jella?'

'Yes, Bingo. I was able to move back time, resize the fish, and help her pass the rocks unhurt,' answered the ecstatic Jella, pointing at the purple fish.

'Wow . . . really?' Bingo looked at the fish and found no marks on her skin. 'You mean, she was injured, and you healed her without actually healing?'

'Bingo, Bingo!' Jella responded ecstatically.

'Really?'

'See, now see, concentrate on that yellow friend, Bingo.' Merjella pointed at a little yellow fish with black dots.

'Okay! Okay! I'm watching.'

Merjella tried to resize her. But nothing happened. She slowly became aggressive in what she was trying to do. She was too concerned that what she was doing should be observable to Bingo. She was not actually focusing enough on the fish.

'Do you see? Do you see that, Bingo? Size shrinking, right?'

'No, Jella! It looks the same.'

Merjella got upset. 'I really did that, Bingo. I just did. I couldn't now! For a moment, I thought I was a jellopus,' said the dejected Merjella.

'You are a jellopus, Jella! Don't lose your heart!' consoled Bingo.

Merjella was not totally convinced by those kind words.

'I've already watched you doing that. When you pulled Marina through the small hole into the tunnel, you actually shrunk her. I saw that, Jella,' explained Bingo.

'Really? I didn't realize that, Bingo.' It was Merjella's turn to find that hard to believe.

'Yes, really. You are a jellopus.' Bingo grinned.

A few feet away from them, there was a shoal of copper-banded butterfly fish feasting on the dirt and food that had settled over a rock. A sailfish slowly positioned herself to prey on them. Both Merjella and Bingo watched curiously. The sailfish had an iridescent blue-striped body with silver dots and also featured a very long and sharp bill. The moment her body colour changed to light blue with yellow stripes, they knew that the hunt was on.

Just when the sailfish, with her wide-opened mouth, was about to attack one of the butterfly fish from behind, the little one's size swelled huge. The stunned predator remained still for a moment as the supposed prey turned back to see what was kissing her tail. That scared the sailfish, and her body colour changed to dark blue. She immediately turned around and took off to escape. The other fish in the group were also shocked to see their swelled-up little mate, and when they became aware that the sailfish was chased away, they started to rejoice the moment, congratulating her. In no time, she regained her original size.

The scared sailfish got behind a rock and started peeping out at the shoal of butterfly fish. Her body colour was rapidly changing out of fear and uncertainty. As the celebrations went on, another sailfish was seen waiting for a chance to attack. But the hiding sailfish signalled her to come to the hideout and promptly communicated what just happened. The news spread rapidly among the fish-eating fish. Soon the bigger and stronger fishes started feeding on seaweeds and zooplanktons instead of other fishes.

Merjella turned back and started moving towards Zypher.

'Stop, Jella! Where are you going?' asked Bingo and moved fast enough to catch up with Merjella's pace.

'Just follow me, Bingo. We are going to storm Zypher and take over it. You saw my might, right?'

'No, no. Stop, Jella! It is not a good idea. You can't do that now, Jella.' Bingo blocked her way.

'Why are you stopping me, Bingo? You saw my power, right? I can do anything now. Let me save my folks.'

'No, Jella. It is true you have the power. But you don't have control over your power. You will be ready only when you have control. You should hone your skills and achieve consistency, Jella. Don't act in hurry,' said Bingo.

'I don't care about control, Bingo. I possess the power, and I am a jellopus. Like what my father, the great Tarjo, predicted, I will win Zypher too. So even though I am not ready, I am destined to. Why not do that this very moment and save my folks right now?' Merjella questioned back.

'Even though your destiny is to win, we cannot take things for granted, Jella. If you wait and deal with it properly, you may achieve this in one moon's time, but your hurried move today might put you in trouble. That, in turn, might delay things a lot even though our victory is destined. Do you want your folks to suffer longer because of your haste? The prescience that we will win is only to help with our morale and not to skip our preparation. No victory is achieved without proper groundwork.' Bingo came up with his prudent thought.

Merjella could not disagree with what Bingo said.

'Save as many lives as you can, Jella. You will get more powerful, and one day you will be invincible. That day, you shall march towards Zypher.'

Merjella remained silent and immersed in some thoughts.

'I need to discover it!'

'What?'

'I have to find out why they stabbed me. I have to go to the land,' said Marina of Merjella.

Bingo could not hear her properly as there was a loud, continuous whizzing noise. They saw the funnel of God yet again, and the tripod legs were trying to get a grip at the seabed. Merjella moved towards the legs, shook it, and pulled violently. Losing its balance, the big boat capsized, and a man fell into the water. The man looked shabby with his beard not properly trimmed, and he was dressed in blue shorts and a yellow shirt. He gasped hard to catch his breath while the fishes thronged around him and kissed him, hailing him as God.

Merjella reached him and turned herself into Marina. She caught hold of him strongly by his neck and made him relax. She asked him to help take her to the land, which he agreed to without much hesitation. Then Merjella bid goodbye to Bingo.

'Stay within this limit, Bingo,' Merjella ordered him while leaving. Then she noticed a few gadgets held by the man. 'What's that, mister?'

'It's an emergency alert switch. It can track me, and also pressing the button will send an alert to my house.'

'And that, mister?' Merjella asked about the one that was clipped to his waist.

He pulled that out and said, 'This one is a walkie-talkie—water-resistant, solar-powered, very high range, and can reach up to several miles.'

Merjella took a close look at the device. 'Why do you need an emergency alert switch when you have a walkie-talkie, mister?'

'My name is Ryan. Ryan Catchmore!'

She showed no response but persisted, 'I asked why.'

'Just a backup, miss,' Ryan said.

'I am Merjella.' She gave both devices to Bingo.

'Always keep these with you, Bingo. When in danger, you press the button. We will be able to save you. And with this one, you can actually speak to me like I am near.'

They then left for the land.

7

RYAN'S GARAGE

Ryan's house was located in a posh locality of the city Blueshells. The independent house was built with stones, and though it looked huge and royal, the lack of maintenance ensured that it remained an eyesore in that area. But inside, the residence was well equipped with state-of-the-art facilities and proved Ryan's mettle at inventions and innovations.

However, it remained untidy all over, indicating the lack of female presence at the home. The major attraction in the house was the giant fish tank made completely of glass and placed in the hall; Ryan raised varieties of fishes in that aquarium with a capacity of about 50,000 litres. It largely served as his testing ground.

From a distance, Merjella spotted a small bell-shaped glass bowl filled with water on a table nearby. To her surprise, Qwerty was inside the bowl.

'This is a rare species thought to be extinct. They are considered the betta fish of the deep oceans. I thought of raising her separately,' said Ryan, seeing her interest in that fish.

Suddenly, Merjella dipped her head into the small bowl. Ryan felt weird watching Merjella's shrunk head and neck inside the bowl while the rest of her body remained in full size outside the water.

'Hi, Qwerty! Are you okay?' Merjella asked Qwerty.

Qwerty was surprised, and she stood shocked.

'I'm okay. But who are you?' she asked back.

'I am Jella!'

'Jella? But what happened to you?'

'I am a jellopus. I can change to any form,' replied Merjella.

Ryan slowly came near the bowl and took a look at what was happening.

'You risked everything just to come and save me. You are an awesome friend, Jella.' Qwerty shed tears.

'You okay?'

'Yes, I am, Jella! But . . .' Qwerty then turned around to show her wound on her rear caused by a needle and pointed at Ryan, who was watching them.

Merjella took her head out and glared at Ryan. He slowly slipped away from the place. She then started touring her new home. After taking stock of various rooms, she finally bumped into the messiest part of the house, and it was Ryan's garage. The garage housed both obsolete and unfinished inventions from Ryan's bandwagon.

Ryan too entered the room with a cup of coffee for his newfound guest. The place always gave Ryan extra energy. The soft-spoken Ryan started to talk about his inventions and also interesting facts behind them. Most of the equipment had gone to rack and ruin, and their purposes and workings can be easily guessed at.

Ryan was well known in that coastal city for his devices made to catch fishes. In fact, the city science museum maintained a separate hall to showcase his inventions. Merjella gazed at the model of the funnel of God in that place for quite a long time.

'This is e-netcatcher. It takes feed from the satellite and has a scanner to locate the place where the density of fish is high in a particular area at a given time.' Showing the three legs of the device, he continued, 'This tripod will help the device to land and rest upright on any surface. After landing, the scent of lilac will be sprayed through this nozzle. Then this funnel-shaped, conical end, which is connected to a suction pump, will start absorbing the fishes that are attracted by the sweet odour. The cone is connected to long pipes that end at this delimeter.' Ryan showed her a small device with a sharp needle attached.

'Delimeter? What does this do?' Merjella enquired.

'It helps with quality check. The needle here will pierce through the fish and measure the deliciousness of the fish by analyzing the quality of the flesh. Those that don't comply will be taken separately and sent back to the water straight away.'

'Oh! That's a nice piece.'

There was a new one in the making that caught her attention too. It did not look like something to catch fishes, and neither could Merjella guess its purpose. She thought it was for some kind of research centre in the sea.

'This is Hotel Gillover. I am working on it to catch bigger fishes. This is designed to look like a fish motel, wherein the fishes will be wooed with drugged, tasty food. Upon consuming it, their oxygen level will drop considerably, and they will look to hit the top for air. The roof of this device is painted to look like it's open, but it leads to a trap.'

'Sounds like a great concept!'

'Yes, it is! We are talking to the state authorities to sanction a sea canal to route all these traps to a common place so that it facilitates large-scale fishing.'

'Oh, nice!' she responded rather superficially.

Ryan understood her remark but looked a little confused whether to carry on or give her a break.

'I am feeling very hungry, Ryan,' Merjella declared, breaking the little pause.

He wasn't very sure of what he could provide her. But he went inside the kitchen to find something for her. Meanwhile, Merjella moved to the hall. While waiting for food, she took out Qwerty from the bowl and placed her on the table. Qwerty's fins enlarged and turned papery and transparent. New little limbs appeared to help her with locomotion. Merjella reached out her forefinger for Qwerty to hold, and then she made her dance as she whistled in a mild tone.

Ryan came back with seafood and joined Merjella to eat.

'It's him, it's him!' yelled Qwerty, pointing at one deliciously roasted fish.

'It's who?'

'We saw him bidding goodbye to his father. We saw him when we saw the funnel of God for the first time.'

'Funnel of God!' exclaimed Ryan.

'Yes! Your e-netcatcher is their funnel of God! And your Hotel Gillover will be called God's restaurant,' added Merjella.

'He prayed to see heaven, but it seems he went to hell and got roasted,' Qwerty expressed her concern.

'Hope he wasn't fried alive,' she added.

'Yes, Qwerty. He is now in the court of God,' Merjella mocked and started tasting the fish.

'You too wanted to see God, right? Here he is—Mr Ryan Catchmore, the god!' Merjella clapped her hands, bowing to Ryan while he blushed uncomfortably. Qwerty felt embarrassed for her earlier decision to fall into the funnel of God.

'Nice food, Ryan. You are a good cook too.' Showing the leftover fish, Merjella said to Qwerty, 'His father should really be proud. He tastes so good. Do you know why that girl was sent back?'

'Which girl?'

'The one who came back crying "*Mummy*, how have I sinned?" in that crowd. That girl! Do you remember?'

'Yes, I do, Jella. She was a cute one. How can I forget her?'

'Do you know why she was sent back?'

'Why?'

'She was found to be not taste-worthy by the *delimeter*. So you better don't lay your lips on her when you get back to the sea. Yuck, yuck!'

'Why will I, Jella? I don't kiss everyone.' After saying that, Qwerty jumped over Merjella and started kissing her cheeks.

'Stop it! Stop it, Qwerty!' Merjella pushed her away. She then arranged the dishes in the table and took the empty plates to the sink.

'Where is Bingo? How is he?' asked Qwerty.

'He is at the sea. As long as the alarm doesn't sound, he should be doing fine,' Merjella replied.

Ryan was overhearing their conversation.

'When are we going back, Jella? I am so eager to see him.'

'Not any time soon, Qwerty. I have work here.'

'Then you didn't come here for me?' Qwerty said sadly.

Merjella felt bad for her.

'You should have brought Bingo along too,' Qwerty said.

'No, we need him there. He will be the right person to re-establish the links Mimico once had. Don't worry, Qwerty. He will be fine. Now we have Ryan, and he will help us fight the malojels and take Zypher back.'

Ryan raised his eyebrows on hearing that from Merjella. He protested, 'I never counted myself in on your war, Merjella.'

'But you promised you would help me.'

'Yes, but not with the silly fish fights. Moreover, I do my living—fishing.'

'What is silly? You live on fishing, and you think the fish world is silly! You need to be taught a lesson, Ryan. But I am not in a mood to see you suffer because of all the favours you have done for me today.'

'I am not scared, Merjella. And I'm a strong man, you should know.'

'Well, well, let's see how strong you are, Ryan!' After saying that, Merjella shrunk Ryan, added gills near his ears, and put him into the giant fish tank. He had his limbs intact and looked human.

Merjella and Qwerty spent some time watching the fishes in the tank. They enjoyed the sight of Ryanfish being chased by bigger and stronger fishes in the tank. The hide and seek he played in that tank decorated with beautiful objects and colourful stones was a treat to watch. After sometime, the tired Ryanfish found a little stone and rested. He seemed to be hungry.

Merjella brought the fishing rod and tied food at the end of the string and started to feed the fishes in the tank. While the other fishes went fighting for the food, Ryanfish was eagerly watching out to see them getting caught in the hook. But to his surprise, the fishes were able to comfortably pull the food and feast on them. Ryanfish soon got convinced to feed himself from the string and went jostling in bravely. Seeing him coming, Merjella attached a hook at the end and served it specially for him. When Ryanfish tried to pounce on the food, the hook pierced through his lips and emerged out through his nose. It was so painful, and he started trembling at the hook.

She then removed and took him away from the water and allowed him to get some air. She pressed his nose and made him suffocate. Somehow he managed to get out of her clutches and jump into the tank, only to race again to safety from the chasing biggies.

Ryanfish started to dash his head at the glass wall, seeking Merjella's attention and signalling her to take him out. He looked very agitated, finding it hard to evade the chasing fishes.

Merjella then came with the e-netcatcher.

'No, no! Not that!' Ryanfish muttered.

Merjella put the device into the huge tank and switched that on. The first to be pulled through the funnel was Ryanfish, and he went through the breath-catching journey through the various tubes connected and finally reached the bed over the top of the delimeter.

'Let's now see what your delimeter score is, Ryan!' said Merjella.

He knew what he was going to experience in the next few seconds, and he shouted for help. But Merjella did not heed him and let the delimeter do the quality check. When the needle pierced, Ryanfish closed his eyes tight, and tears oozed out at the deep pain.

Though Ryanfish was crying, Merjella chose not to show any pity for his indomitable gestures made earlier, and she moved ahead with her plans. She picked him out and passed him to Qwerty, who tonsured his head and applied paste made of chilli powder and other spices on his body. Ryanfish's heartbeat kept accelerating. He was impatiently looking for ways to escape, but it was impossible with Merjella and Qwerty having fun watching him constantly.

Merjella poured oil in a pan and heated that up. When the oil started to heat up, she caught hold of the seasoned Ryanfish by his one leg and took him close to being put into the boiling oil to fry. He was held upside down such that his head was very near the frying pan. He bent and clung tightly to her fingers and begged her to spare him for whatever she would order.

Merjella was convinced that he would never protest again. She pulled him away from the pan. He was brought back to his original form. Even as he was regaining his breath, Merjella disappeared right in front of him. He stood frightened for a while before moving slowly to reach his bedroom. He thought of resting a while, but Merjella was already occupying the space. She was more tired and deserved the comfy bed more than Ryan did.

8

ROSY PARKER

'Miss you a lot, Bingo. You should've come here too,' spoke Qwerty over the walkie-talkie, seated comfortably on a specially made small cushion placed on the couch.

Merjella and Qwerty were talking to Bingo while Ryan was watching television. Ryan was in his casual shorts and printed colourful shirt, lying flat on the couch and holding the remote control for the television. It was then that the doorbell rang. All of them became alert and looked at the door.

Jerking out of the sofa, Ryan wondered, 'How did I forget?'

'Forget what, Ryan? Who is at the door?'

'It should be the Parkers! We were supposed to have dinner tonight. Nothing is ready now.'

'Don't worry, I will take care of that,' assured Merjella.

'But I don't want them to see you. Not her. Definitely not Rosy Parker.'

'Why so? What harm will she bring?'

As they were discussing that, the bell started to ring impatiently.

'Rosy Parker is a newsmonger. You have to go hide, Merjella, please,' Ryan requested of her meekly.

'Okay, Ryan! I will go invisible, and Qwerty too.'

'No! I will stay like this,' protested Qwerty, and she went jumping and hopping into the kitchen.

Ryan opened up the door for his guests, feigning to have just woken up from sleep. Rosy was surprised to see his head tonsured, and she gave him a strange look. They then rushed in. The Parkers included David Parker, Rosy Parker, and their eight-year-old son, James Parker.

'What happened to you, Ryan? Why did you suddenly shave your head? Are you all right, Ryan?' Rosy gave an interrogatory stare right at the doorstep. 'Oh, look at you! Poor boy! What is this?' She was shocked at seeing the needle injury on his nose caused by the fishing hook. 'How did this happen, Ryan?'

'What?' Ryan rubbed his left forefinger on his face to find out what she was talking about.

'The holes on your lips and nose. Something's wrong with you, Ryan. You should see a psychologist.'

'Oh, that's because of the needle. I didn't know it was on the bed.'

'You are mourning way too much, Ryan. You should socialize,' suggested Rosy.

'I am just tired, Rosy! Had a long day,' explained Ryan.

They all went straight to his workshop as that fascinated them all.

'It is still in the same stage, Ryan! What happened to you?' David Parker asked.

'You still seem to be mourning Billy's death. Why don't you find another one for your fabrication needs?' suggested Rosy.

Ryan was not eager to reply to her. Meanwhile, James was tired from running around in the room and playing with his favourite remote-controlled car. He later came to his mother and asked for water. But then Rosy was not prepared to leave in the middle of the conversation and asked him to fetch it himself.

She continued, 'I know a very talented girl who can help you in your fabrication work. I will be able to introduce her at our mayor's birthday bash this Saturday.'

'I don't think someone can work with me like Billy did. He could easily read me and my needs. Poor soul. I miss him a lot, Rosy.'

'This girl is a real talent, Ryan. Trust me.'

'I don't think anyone can replace him, Rosy. That too, a girl! No, Rosy. Don't trouble yourself. I appreciate your help though.'

'It's okay, Ryan! But what made you think a girl cannot do certain things?'

Mr Parker intruded what he felt to be a mind-numbing conversation, 'You ladies can't even park a car properly, Rosy.'

'Why do guys always think that only driving cars and making machines mean skill? How about you guys try your hand in cooking?' While she was saying that, there was a pleasant aroma spreading in the room. 'What is that, Ryan?'

She rushed straight into the kitchen to see the food waiting to nourish their appetite. She could not wait any longer, and the dining table was set in a hurry. Everyone enjoyed the meal, and compliments kept pouring in for Ryan.

'We had dinner with you before, but never have you made anything this good. Never did I think you could cook like this, Ryan,' remarked Rosy in excitement.

'You can see now that men can cook too,' said David.

'This is proof enough, Ryan. If a man can do a girl's job better, then so is the other way round. The world is fast changing, Ryan. You should consider my option. We will meet Sandy Wonka in the gathering this Saturday.'

Suddenly, the main door opened, and Merjella came in, carrying a bag full of vegetables and groceries. For a moment, Ryan stood still in shocked silence.

Merjella was in her usual outfit, a gown made of transparent pink fabric with curls of thick pink threads running through the dress and forming designs similar to the arms of an octopus. She looked like an angel in pink.

'Meet my new maid.' Ryan introduced her to the Parkers without much hesitation.

'How sweet! We were just appreciating the food and were in the dark about who had made it this good. What is your name?' Rosy asked.

'Merjella!'

'Merjella, a maid. Sounds like mermaid. You look like one too,' complimented Rosy.

'Thank you, Mrs . . .'

'Parker. Rosy Parker.'

'Hope you enjoyed the meal, Mrs Parker.'

'Absolutely, Merjella. So . . . where did you come from, mermaid? The sea?' Mrs Parker asked wittily.

'She is from Karzha,' intruded Ryan.

'Where did you find her, Ryan?' asked David to Ryan.

'She was raised in an orphanage. A common friend requested me to lend a hand to the poor girl. And here she is.'

'Never knew you were this generous, Ryan. You are soon going to have another lady to assist you. I think you would not be able to refuse my request like you didn't with your other friend,' Rosy said.

Ryan did not seem to have any other option but to oblige her, like Mr Parker would do most of the time.

'So where is she staying, Mr Catchmore!' asked David.

'Well, she is staying here. Uh . . . I mean, this is a temporary arrangement—just until she gets a suitable accommodation.'

'Are you looking?' Rosy got inquisitive.

'No. No. Pardon me. What did you ask?' Ryan hesitated.

'Are you looking for a house? For her?'

'Yes, right, Rosy.'

She then turned to Merjella and said, 'You may also join the party, Miss Mer . . . maid!'

'Merjella,' Ryan said helpfully.

Rosy smiled at both Ryan and Merjella. She kept reminding them to join the party at every opportunity the conversations gave. They stayed late in the night and left around midnight.

9

QWERTY AND THE RING

The Parkers reached home. They were very tired after a long day. They headed straight to bed as soon as they changed. The family had a large, spacious bedroom with a bed big enough for all the Parkers to park in for a night's sleep.

Rosy tucked James in, and she lay in between the senior and junior Parkers. She then stroked James's head gently and tapped his chest. That was her customary effort to put him to sleep. Her stroking arm became still after some time as she fell asleep. In the dead of the night, James woke up and quietly removed her hand from him. Picking up his overcoat, James prowled to the kitchen without knowing he had alerted his mother on the process. As the kitchen light was lit, Rosy peeped from outside the kitchen door to see what he was up to.

The moment James pulled out Qwerty from his pocket, all hell broke loose as Rosy started bawling at him. She had no idea about what he was holding in his hand. She was shocked as well as frightened of that new species, but soon she came to her senses.

'What is this creature?'

'Don't know, Mom! I found it in Mr Ryan's kitchen.'

'Oh my god! Why did you bring it here?' She dialled Ryan. 'Ryan! What is going on in your place? Have you started adopting strange creatures?'

'Did you see Qwerty, Rosy?'

'So it has a name too?'

'Where did you see her? Where is she? Do you have any information, Rosy?'

'It is right here—with my son, James!'

'Thank God! We were looking for her all over here. You please keep her safe, Rosy. I will come and pick her up first thing in the morning.'

'Sure, Ryan! Goodnight!' Rosy then turned to James and asked, 'Why did you bring it, James?' She gave a close look at Qwerty. 'So weird! Legged little fishy creature! Looks like some insect with flesh, James.'

'I saw it walking like we do. I saw it holding a cashew nut like we do with our hands.'

'So?'

'I thought we can use it to bring back the ring you lost, the one that slipped here!' James pointed at the kitchen sink.

'Oh, poor boy! It is lost, James! Don't even touch that insect again. Now get back to bed.'

'Mom, I don't like it when Dad screams at you!' The boy broke into tears.

Mrs Parker was so moved, and she hugged him before sending him back to bed. Rosy then got hold of Qwerty and placed her inside an empty fruit basket. She did not forget to wrap her up with some old clothes and left her in the kitchen itself. She again tucked James and lay down on her usual place on the bed. The senior Parker did not show any sign of unrest while the whole incident happened.

The next morning, before anyone in the home was up, the doorbell rang. Rosy, half asleep, went to answer the door. Ryan and Merjella were seen waiting at the door on that cold day. She beamed her usual smile and let them in.

'Sorry to disturb you, Rosy. But Qwerty is very important to her,' Ryan explained.

Rosy went into the kitchen to pick up Qwerty while Ryan and Merjella waited on the couch. Rosy kept her home very tidy and had photographs of precious moments decorating the walls. Her wedding picture showed the kind of craze she had for jewels. She was seen decorated with a diamond necklace and sparkling earrings. And the wedding ring easily topped the attention-pullers.

Inside the kitchen, Rosy was busy searching for Qwerty. She was not to be found in the fruit basket, where she had been kept the previous night. As Rosy informed Ryan, he panicked, and so did Merjella. They all hurried to the kitchen.

'James! Why would he take her?' grunted Ryan.

'Oh, don't blame the kid, Ryan. Poor boy wanted to recover my ring that fell into the hole in the sink.' Rosy moved on to make coffee for the guests.

Merjella shrunk herself, and with her wings, she took off into that small pipeline. It did not take her long to spot Qwerty. She was standing there, shivering and sticking to one side of the pipe. She was frozen in the cold.

'What are you doing here?'

'I came to find the ring for Mrs Parker.'

'How long have you been here? Did you get the ring?'

'No, Jella. I couldn't climb back up as well. The pipe is slippery.'

'How long have you searched for this ring?' Merjella asked her again, highlighting with a beam of light from her index finger the ring that was lying very close to Qwerty.

'Oh, Jella! I was searching for this all night. It was dark, and I couldn't see it at all.'

'It's okay, Qwerty. Pick that up and climb now. The pipe is a little dry now.'

Qwerty tried climbing, but it was still sticky for her.

Seeing Qwerty struggling, Merjella asked, 'What do you think the wings I have given you are for?'

'These thin fins? I thought they are for balancing myself while walking.'

'Wiggle your wings, and try flying, Qwerty!'

Qwerty was so excited and started fluttering her wings. But every time she put pressure down and tried to take off with a jump, she only fell back. She was not able to fly properly and became a laughing stock for Merjella.

'Leave the ring, and try flying, Qwerty. The ring is too heavy for you to fly with,' suggested Merjella.

When Qwerty tried without the ring, she could fly but not swiftly. Still, she managed to reach the top and was just a little hop away to reach the other end and out on the sink. Holding on to the grill in the sink's hole, Qwerty turned back to Merjella and asked for the ring.

'It is right up there, Qwerty.'

She found the ring near her. She picked that up and gathered her breath to take her final hop to other side of the grill. But a flood of water gushed in at her, and she started falling upside down before Merjella caught her and took her to safety.

Inside the home, Ryan was upset about the tap being opened. 'Why would you open the tap, Rosy? You might have killed Merjella.'

'Merjella? Where is she?' Rosy looked around.

'I mean Qwerty. She will drown if she is inside. Use the other tap.' Saying this, Ryan locked the tap of the sink.

'Okay, fine! But where is Merjella?'

'She looked worried. She might have gone to the garden to get fresh air, Rosy.'

James came walking in, half sleep.

'Mom! I saw Qwerty bringing back the ring in my dream.'

Rosy held on to him and said, 'Oh, sweetheart, forget about the ring.'

Meanwhile, Qwerty managed to fly back to the top of the pipeline and picked up the ring and successfully crossed the grill to see the kitchen side.

'Mom!' screamed James in delight. 'It has brought your ring back!'

Rosy was surprised to see Qwerty back with her ring. Ryan lifted Qwerty and handed over the ring to Rosy.

'Okay, Rosy. We will go now.'

'Wait, Ryan. Coffee is ready. Let me call Merjella to join us.'

Ryan sat down in the hall while Rosy went to the garden to call Merjella. James was playing with Qwerty when David joined them for coffee. Soon, Rosy was back with Merjella. They all enjoyed coffee.

'Mom! Why is she called Qwerty?'

Quick-witted, exceptional, rational thinker, yo, said Qwerty in her mind.

'*Qwerty* means "something that looks like in order but, in reality, is not". You see those letters in that order in a keyboard, but they are not in that order in the alphabet.'

Qwerty looked so disappointed with such an explanation.

Rosy continued saying, 'So it should mean something misleading. It may look like a friend, but it is not. You should stop liking it, James.' She then enquired of Ryan, 'Where did you find it, Mr Catchmore?'

'Merjella brought her along. She discovered her in the sea and brought her to me,' Ryan replied to her question.

'What are you planning to do with it? It looks like a new species. It may be alien too. Don't you think you should hand it over to the government?'

'Well, yes. I am planning to find her genetic combinations. It might be useful if we can spot the exact gene that is the reason for those amazing features,' explained Ryan.

'Amazing features? Huh! What are they?'

Ryan got hold of Qwerty and let Rosy take a look at her. 'Do you see that she has hands and legs with fingers like a squirrel and has a body like a fish and also has wings?'

'Yes, I can see that.'

'Now, watch when I throw her in the air.' Saying this, Ryan actually threw Qwerty up in the air. 'You can see her fly.'

Qwerty took flight and landed on Merjella's shoulder.

'That's wonderful!'

'That is not all. When I put her in the water, she will start swimming.'

'Awesome creature, Ryan. Now I understand what you are planning to do—single out the gene responsible and mix that with a human and develop a superhuman. Wow! What a creator you are!' Rosy expressed her faint praise on him.

'Exactly, Rosy! You are smart! We have things to do now. We shall catch up later!'

Ryan and Merjella left the Parkers' residence with Qwerty.

10

Mayor's Party

Jack Smith was the mayor of Blueshells. He was a very popular figure in the city and politically powerful as well. Nobody in the city could remember the last time he was called by his original name. The word *mayor* became synonymous with him for more than two decades in the city.

He had this tradition of throwing a huge party marking his birthday every year. Usually, it would be the first Saturday following his birthday. That year, his birthday happened to fall on a Saturday, and hence the celebrations were set to go overboard.

Usually, hundreds of high-profile citizens in the city, along with chief guests from other places, would gather to greet him. He made it a habit to personally greet each and every person at the party—from one-year-olds to ton-year-olds—with no discrimination whatsoever. It was considered to be the best occasion for introducing new people to him as well as to the gathering.

The first to arrive at the party were undoubtedly the Parkers. They managed to beat the second best by almost twenty minutes. That was the most eagerly awaited occasion in Rosy's calendar, and she would never even consider giving that a miss even if she was warming her deathbed.

Her agenda that night was clearly cut out—to introduce Sandy Wonka and Merjella to as many as she could. And she was ready and up for the task. And of course, she was looking to source some rumours too.

With the advent of the vibrant atmosphere, guests started to fill the foyer slowly but steadily. The party started to get louder and louder as more and more joined in.

Before Rosy could put out an eager eye on the entrance, Sandy arrived. It was perfect timing, and she was straight away greeted by Rosy and was taken a full round among the distinctive people to seek blessings. She graduated recently and was a daughter of the famous physicist in the city, Thomas Wonka. He was not known to socialize, and it was more than appropriate for Sandy to choose Rosy to launch her social life.

Ryan was never known for timekeeping. He too was not a socializing type, but Rosy had already made umpteen calls in the last couple of days for him to be present. Gracing the occasion with his presence was itself a big thing, and he had no intention of making his presence felt earlier. Rosy had to have all eyes on the gate for him, and finally he arrived.

He came alone. Knowing Ryan well, Rosy was indeed sure that he would not bring Merjella to the party. She was glad that at least he came. She could not wait to introduce Sandy to him.

'Miss Sandy Wonka! Specialized in casting and moulding techniques. Masters degree from the University of Pynto. This is the girl I was talking about, Ryan!'

Ryan greeted her formally.

'She is cute, isn't she?' asked Qwerty to Merjella.

Oh, yes, Qwerty and Merjella were indeed present at the party! They both were in the size of ants.

'More than me?' asked Merjella.

'Yes, cuter than you! But you are beautiful, Jella.'

'You can distinguish between cute and beautiful?'

'Yes, of course. Cute is Sandy, and beautiful is Jella! As simple as that!'

'You are getting smarter. Pretty smart, huh!'

'So pretty is Qwerty, right? Pretty Qwerty!'

'Exactly. So Ryan will have Beauty, Cutie, and Pretty at home soon!'

They then focused on listening to the conversation between Rosy and Ryan.

'This Monday is auspicious, Ryan. I shall take her to your place,' Rosy said.

Ryan Catchmore nodded in acceptance.

'Why isn't Merjella here?'

'She has a bad migraine. She couldn't even get up from bed.'

'Oh, sad! Headache is not a good reason to miss this place. As long as you are not dead, you should be here. Such is the atmosphere and the people you meet here,' Rosy opined.

'I wonder if this party will happen at all if Rosy is no more!' commented Qwerty.

'I wonder if Rosy will live at all if this party is not going to happen any more! Long live Mr Mayor!' said Merjella.

'Where is the birthday boy, Jella?'

'Mmmm . . . Come, let's find him!'

The tiny figures on the party floor moved from there to find Mr Jack Smith, the host of the day.

David Parker soon joined Ryan and Rosy.

'Hello, Mr Catchmore. Hope you are having a great time!' enquired Mr Parker.

'Well, yeah. When Rosy is around, you can't expect otherwise, can you?' Ryan shot back.

'No comments. Absolutely no comments!' David Parker said.

David hardly spoke when Rosy was around. And the easy way to shut his mouth was to refer to her name in a conversation. Ryan had practised that skill to perfection. He knew he could not silence Rosy, but he knew how to extract half the relief by silencing her better half.

Sandy Wonka was gifted with a sweet voice too, and Rosy was well aware of that. Naturally, Wonka had to take the stage for a karaoke performance. When she was singing, Merjella and Qwerty danced happily. They enjoyed it very much. Sandy also impressed the gathering with her keyboarding skills. It was Ryan who was most impressed with her, and he was convinced that she was a talent.

Mr Jack Smith arrived and started his routine of welcoming and socializing with each and every attendee.

Seeing Jack Smith, Merjella got palpitations. She could not stand firmly, and she collapsed near the leg of a table that hosted an array of wine glasses. Qwerty was shocked and was out of ideas of how to help. She did not know what had happened to Merjella.

She ran back and forth without knowing what to do. She rushed to Ryan and tried to get his attention. The noisy atmosphere made her difficult job impossible. She tried scratching his legs, but his alcohol level had already risen to a level that he could not feel a thing. She flew to reach his nose and tried to get his attention. Qwerty's efforts failed to bring him out of his stupor. Worse still, he hit her like he would do to any other fly sitting on his face. That hurt her wings, and she fell down.

Agitated, Qwerty tottered to reach Merjella. She slowly tried to climb the table leg near her. It was vertical and steep, but with much difficulty, she managed to climb to the top. She wanted to push a glass of wine directly down Merjella's face so that she would come to consciousness. But the filled-up bottles were heavy, and she could not push them even slightly. She looked around, and there was a bottle with a few sips left. She went near it and started to push it with her full might. But she only succeeded in shaking the bottle. She realized she could put in extra effort by running from a distance and throwing herself at the bottle.

So she took few steps away from the bottle and took a deep breath, but she was not ready to do that. She wanted to see the height from where she would fall, so she went near the edge of the table and looked down. It was pretty high, and she tried to take a close look at Merjella. She thought she would not need to risk that if Merjella was already up. But Merjella was still in a faint. She again took a few steps back and took a deep breath. She started to run and pick up speed. Just when she took off to kick the bottle, a servant, on his duty of picking empty glasses, took the bottle, and Qwerty could not halt herself in mid-air. In the next second, she was on the floor.

She did not lose confidence. In fact, she could not afford to. She had to help Merjella. She got up and climbed to the top of the table again. She found stirrers and some corks scattered there. She brought a cork and positioned it a little away from the wine glass. Then she picked up a stirrer and placed the flat side under the glass leg and used the cork like a fulcrum. She went to the other end and began to jump to catch hold of the end. And when she successfully did, the flat end of the stirrer lifted the bottom of the wine glass, and it fell. Fortunately, it fell near Merjella and was enough to wet her face and bring her back to consciousness.

It did not take long for Merjella to realize where she was. With a touch, she healed Qwerty's wings. She, along with Qwerty, went invisible but back to their original sizes. They went out of the party area to the inside of the house. Merjella walked in as if she knew the place very well.

She took Qwerty to a bedroom, and they found a bag there. Merjella hurriedly searched the bag and then the room, but it was in vain. She searched other rooms too but got nothing that would please her. Qwerty looked at her, puzzled. They left the room, carrying the bag, and went to the party hall.

Before leaving the place, the invisible Merjella went near the mayor and, into his ear, said, 'The boss is going to be very furious.' She left straight for Ryan's car and waited.

Frightened by the voice, Jack Smith left the scene urgently. After he left, the crowd soon dispersed.

11

DEIMOS BETRAYED

When they got home, Merjella sat on her bed with the bag unzipped and everything pulled out.

'What is this bag, Merjella?' asked Ryan Catchmore.

'This is our bag, Ryan. But I didn't recover our systems and research papers. They are missing. It seems they were stolen.'

'Looks like your memory is back, Merjella. Are you able to identify yourself?'

'Yes, Ryan. I can remember some. My name is Marina Jalencia. I think I was an inventor. I am not sure what my inventions were and what I was working on. Maybe if I find those papers, I might have a better idea. It should be more valuable, and as far as I can remember, it was being put into wrong use. I should stop that also.'

'What else can you remember Merjella? Let me see if I can help you.'

'I remember the confrontation I had with my husband, Deimos, Ryan.' Merjella began to disclose all she could recollect to him.

It was a usual waiting night for Marina at her posh residential apartment in the city of Kreppo. Deimos was yet to return from work even as the clock ran well past his usual homecoming hour. There were no signs of him arriving, and he was not picking up his mobile either.

It was then that the doorbell rang impatiently. After a peep through the eyehole of the door, she opened it. It was Deimos rushing in.

'Come on, honey! Pack everything!' he ordered hurriedly.

'What? What is the matter, Deimos?'

'Our pro-dog was caught by police. They are investigating,' replied Deimos.

Marina looked confused. 'What's wrong with that? Did she harm anyone?'

'No, baby! We don't have much time to discuss that. We will leave now, and we will get protection from our boss.'

'No, Deimos, I am not going anywhere. I need to know what has happened. Why is pro-dog being held?'

'Honey! They suspect that she was used for drug trafficking.'

'Oh, no. Not right, dear. We will go and explain to them.'

'No, darling, it is not gonna happen. We can't explain. She was indeed used for trafficking. My boss used it for that. I'm sorry, baby. We don't have much choice. Come on. Pack up,' pleaded Deimos.

Marina was in deep shock to learn that.

'Is that what our brainchild has been used for? A great concept of a programmable living creature was wasted on drug trafficking? Oh my god! You are not a good person, Deimos. You are not!' screamed Marina.

'Dear . . . dear . . . even I was not aware of that, dear. Trust me. Like you trusted me, I trusted my boss, and even I was shocked to learn that.'

'Then why do you want to go to him, Deimos? He betrayed us.'

'He is the only one who can help us now, dear. Only he can protect us.'

'No, dear! Let us surrender and turn him in, Deimos. Law will accept us more than him.'

'He can't be brought to law, Marina. He is big. He is influential. We just can't bring him down.'

'Then we will find a different place, Deimos. But not to him. We know he is bad. We better not go to him.'

'Okay, fine! You pack our things. I shall secure our research works. We will leave at once.'

'Where to, baby?'

'Somewhere, honey! Maybe . . . Blueshells. I have friends there who can help us start a new lease of life. Come on, dear!'

Convinced and forward-looking, Marina started packing necessary things. The doorbell rang again. The ring of the bell in the stillness of the night startled both of them. Deimos gathered his courage and went to answer the door.

'Oh! John and Mike! I'm afraid it may take more time for us to pack. Please wait in the parking lot.'

John and Mike nodded and moved.

Then Deimos seemed to change his mind, and he popped out of the door and called them. As they turned back to listen to what he had to say, Deimos said, 'John, it may take at least half an hour. Why don't you guys chill out at the bar nearby for some time?'

That was the first time Marina was seeing John and Mike. Their physique suggested they were the boss's men sent to escort them. They were well dressed in black, and they hardly smiled. Whatever they were, Marina wished she would never see them again in her life. Having them around would give one the feeling of a gangster. Not many would fancy that, and it was definitely not the type that Marina was.

'Come on, baby. Hurry up. We will have to leave before they notice us.'

'I'm ready, honey! You have to finish your work.'

'I'm finished too. We shall move then.'

The once-celebrated scientists were on the run. They may soon be declared outlaws. Once they got out of the apartment, they boarded a taxi and sped away. They reached the city railway junction. As they entered, there was an announcement going on for the next train to Blueshells.

'I guess we are gonna make it quite easily, darling,' remarked Deimos.

Marina smiled and kissed him. They bought tickets and got into the train in time. To enable a comfortable journey, they reserved themselves berths—lower and upper in that two-tiered compartment. As they moved into their compartment and spotted their berths, they deposited their luggage at a safe position. They exchanged relieved smiles at each other. Deimos then lifted her up and helped her lie on the upper berth, and he stood watching her.

'I don't like this life, Deimos, this fugitive life. I am not made for this. But still I prefer this over the life we were living since our marriage. You hardly found time for me. Sometimes I would feel that you did not love me any more. But this day is special to me, Deimos. I'm being loved. I'm being listened to.' Saying this, Marina leaned over to kiss Deimos. They kissed for a while.

'I've always loved you, honey. Pity we could invent all impossible things to ease everyone's lives and save time, but not invent a way to show our love without the need to invest time.'

'You are not a love material, Deimos, are you? Love and time are inseparable. Love grows with time we spend together. Even when not near each other, the time we spend thinking of the other helps keep our love alive.'

'But then something has to be done to make it easy, honey!'

'Poor Deimos! Depth of love can be measured by the way it is expressed in difficult situations. Why ask for ease, silly?'

Deimos could only smile to cover his embarrassment on his ignorance about love.

'Sleep, baby!' Deimos brought his right hand over her forehead and near her eyes and slowly moved down towards her nose so that she would close her eyes and start to rest. And the approach seemed to work.

'Have you informed your friend there about our arrival?' questioned Marina with her eyes closed.

'No, dear! Just chose not to disturb him now. We will trouble him early in the morning. You have some peace now, baby. Sleep.' Deimos tried rubbing her shoulder gently. The change of tactics seemed to be working well. Marina smiled with her eyes shut.

'I can't sleep when you are standing and staring at me like this,' she confessed, and Deimos moved, planting a goodnight kiss on her cheeks.

The journey to Blueshells was a one-night journey covering a little above a thousand miles from Kreppo. They were able to get a good sleep after a good end to that eventful day.

Deimos was the first to wake up to the new day. He watched Marina sleeping for a while. He did not want to disturb the peace he saw in her. As scheduled, the train should reach Blueshells in another thirty minutes, and he learnt from the fellow passengers that the train was on time.

He then brushed his teeth and washed his face and got ready for the new day. He woke Marina up. She beamed a sweet good-morning smile at him.

'Has your friend been informed?'

'You look too concerned, baby. There won't be any issue getting there. Relax, baby. I don't want to make calls from my mobile. We will do that from the booth in the station. It would be a matter of a few minutes for him to get us picked up.'

Like he said, they found themselves with a comfortable escort within minutes of him making a call from the railway station. They were taken straight to the house of Jack Smith, who was called mayor by everyone.

They were shown to a room. It was elegantly crafted, and interiors were designed with a lavender theme. It was very vibrant and, at the same time, cool on the eyes too. It had a big cot with a spring mattress to rest on. The bath had a large shower panel, in which Marina spent a considerable time washing herself. As they got ready, they were invited for breakfast with the mayor himself.

At the dining table, the mayor's family and the Jalencia couple exchanged pleasantries. The mayor assured unconditional support to them.

'You must relax for a few days before starting it afresh, Mr Deimos. I recommend that you tour the places around. As you know, this is one of the finest tourist destinations in the entire world.' He called for one of his staff, and he arrived.

'Ramon! This is Mr Deimos. I want you to help him explore our city.'

The mayor then turned to Deimos and said, 'He will help you for the next two days. On Sunday, I shall take you to the sea, to some place you haven't imagined you would be able to see in life. That's a promise.'

Back in the room, Deimos and Marina relaxed.

'Finally we are at the right place, Deimos. You do have good friends,' acknowledged Marina.

'I too feel so. I have been missing you for so long, Marina. My heart says that we are going to have our honeymoon followed by a perfect life here.'

They were soon in a great mood, forgetting their past and forgetting the fact that the past might have a future. But brave men take things one by one, and that was why they are brave.

As instructed, Ramon took them to the beautiful parts of the land. Forts, palaces, galleries, and museums were major attractions in that city, apart from the beaches.

Marina always loved palaces, and so did Deimos. She would always go for the life of a princess, but then who in this world would not? Royal life was the reason for her obsession in palaces while Deimos had a strange craving for power. He wanted to be a king so he would not feel weak. All throughout his life, he had to struggle past frustrations. He had worked very hard to reach where he was then.

It was Sunday morning. Deimos and Marina were still lying on the bed, but they were both awake.

'How does it feel being here, milady? Better?'

'Not just better, milord. Milady is feeling out of this world. In the last two days, the love milord had shown was too much to be had for a lifetime.'

They both kissed each other rather passionately.

'So milady seems to be ready for the little adventure at sea.'

'Hmm . . . what could that be, Deimos?'

'What?'

'That which we are going to see, that which we haven't imagined we would see in life. What could that be, Deimos?'

'I am like you, Marina—clueless! But I guess we may be going scuba diving. That's only my guess, but don't be disappointed if that won't happen.'

'No! No! Anything will be fine, dear. When you are near, there is nothing that will make me disappointed.'

The couple got ready, and they were soon heading for the beach with the mayor. He commanded huge respect in that city, which was quite visible. As they reached the sea, there was a special cruiser waiting for them. The couple took the seats in the open to have a fine view of the sea.

'How was your stay, Mr Deimos?' asked Jack Smith, the mayor.

'Fine! Pretty fine, Mr Mayor!' came the reply.

The boat traversed some distance away from the shore, and all they could see was water. Everything looked blue.

'Blue is a fascinating colour. Isn't it, Mr Deimos?'

'Yes, it is. But my favourite is red.'

'Red indicates heat and violence—the colour of blood. Looks like two days weren't enough to bring calmness to your mind, Mr Deimos.' After saying that, Smith looked at Marina and asked, 'What is your favourite colour, madam?'

'Green!' She was quick with her answer as if she had long been expecting the question.

'That's a lovely choice, lady—the colour of life. I wish you a long life, Mrs Deimos,' said Smith, and he turned slightly to look at Deimos and continued, 'Of course, with your beloved husband.'

That was the lighter moment in that lonely atmosphere.

'I would like to use the restroom, mayor,' said Deimos, and Jack Smith asked one of his men to show him the way. Deimos was taken into the room in that luxurious cruiser.

All Marina could see was blue water and blue sky. She could see some fishes that swam near the surface. Birds were sighted too. And when she started to employ her inspecting eyes to see more details, she heard a loud pistol shot. She was shocked, but the mayor smiled at her.

'Looks like the boss is furious!' he observed.

'The boss!' Marina broke down crying as she got up from her seat. She rushed towards the room, crying, 'Deimos! Deimos!'

Marina was unable to believe they were betrayed, and soon two men were seen coming out of the room. They were John and Mike, whom she had not wanted to see again in her life. They were fast approaching her, and she rightly realized she was to be shown what cannot be seen in life—death. She hurriedly moved backwards to the corner of the cruiser.

Jack Smith was absolutely enjoying the scene. John had already wielded out a sharp knife from the pocket of his black coat. Before Mike could take a rigid hold of Marina, she started to slip from the boat, yet John managed to stab her back and tear her skin. Blood spilled fast in that huge mass of water, creating a red stain in that beautiful blue sea.

'The boss is going to be very furious!' remarked Smith again. That was exactly what Marina heard last.

John and Mike watched the place where she fell, and they smiled.

'What's there to be amused about, gentlemen?' questioned Smith.

'Sharks are nearby, Mr Mayor!'

Merjella's eyes welled up while she was narrating that.

'What happened afterwards is well known to you, Ryan!'

'Yes, right! So you have never seen the boss?'

'No. I don't think so. Maybe I might have seen him. I should find out what happened earlier in my life. I can't cast my mind beyond the most recent events now!'

'I guess the boss is someone close to our mayor. We can find out if we tail his activities, Merjella.'

'Yes, Ryan. I too feel so. And we have to find my research papers before they are put into wrong use.'

'I don't think we can do that. You just said they were already used for trafficking. Do you remember what pro-dog is?'

'All I can remember is that they are programmable animals, maybe in dog form.'

'Sounds like a robot.'

'I don't think so. I guess they are much more than that—maybe real dogs that are programmed using some chips.'

'That sounds hazardous, not just dangerous, Merjella. And that too in evil hands.'

'True, Ryan. We will have to do what we can to save the world, Catchmore. I am glad I am not just Marina now.'

'Right! Your powers are boundless, and nothing can be a bigger threat to humankind as long as you are alive, Merjella!'

12

FABRICATOR AT WORK

Even before daylight knocked Ryan's sleep off, Rosy, along with Sandy Wonka, knocked on his doors on that breezy Monday morning. It was only eight, and Ryan gave a not-so-friendly look at Rosy, which she negotiated with a care-not attitude.

'The auspicious time is running out,' Rosy said to no one. She went straight to the kitchen and made coffee for everyone at home. Then, in that brief time she stayed, she did not fail to conduct her usual rumour session at the coffee table.

Though not many preferred to work with Ryan Catchmore, Sandy specifically wanted to. That was why she was pushing Rosy Parker hard to get that job. For Sandy, Catchmore's was the right place to earn more expertise in her field as he was known to be a man of fascinating ideas.

Ryan Catchmore—his odd second name was not something that he had acquired from his ancestors. In fact, he was an orphan brought up in an orphanage located close to the beach of Seashells. His childhood days were spent mostly with the local fishermen, who relentlessly challenged one another in going for the largest catch. The sportive aggression they showed while fishing and the festivities later on in the nights had always fascinated Ryan. He slowly started getting involved in their profession and teaming up with them. He used to come up with some novel ideas that would eventually increase the catch, and hence he was named Catchmore by his fishermen friends.

His talent caught the attention of an heirless shipping baron, Mr Edward Grover. He adopted Ryan when he was fourteen, and Ryan established the company Catchmore Fishing Equipments (CFE). The old man did not live long to see his investment on Ryan yield rich dividends. After his demise, Ryan transferred Edward's shipping business to the charity which oversaw the orphanage he came from. He took Grover's home and the CFE business for himself.

By that time, CFE became a deteriorating business with Ryan's ideas failing to strike a chord with consumers. He did not have enough technical know-how on giving wings to his ideas. It was at that juncture that Billy joined CFE with the arrangement that he would acquire half the share in the business if his association with Ryan would help turn around the prospects of the company. He was to provide fabrication assistance and thereby give flight to Ryan's wings.

Despite both of them being labelled mediocre achievers in their respective fields, together they succeeded in quick time. There were several reasons attributed to their astonishing success.

Firstly, they were both bachelors and had always remained so. That enabled them to invest dedication along with hard work and proficiency into their projects. Billy moved in with Ryan as they got busier with assignments. They hardly made any new friends for themselves as they were both not known for socializing. That easily made them share the same set of dreams as well, and that could be counted as a big factor in paving the way for their triumphant journey.

But then the journey was not as smooth as it was described. They did have initial hiccups. As both were awful at communication, blunders were aplenty to start with. They both did not restrain from blaming each other for their mistakes.

'You have an awesome earpiece, old man,' Ryan would comment about Billy's listening capability. Billy was more than a decade older than Ryan.

'You have a wonderful mouthpiece, young chap,' Billy would hit back.

And there would be a short break. They later would patch up and work that out again—with more clarity. That was possible as both were not in any sort of demand in the market. Naturally, they had to settle with each other's assistance.

It was about fifteen years back when they started off with a device called multi-hooks, which was one of the very few failures for Ryan and Billy together. Ryan complained that Billy failed to make the device like he designed and that he was not respecting the specifications provided to him. Billy had made all strings of the same length with hooks attached at the ends, and that made winding and unwinding very complicated. Ryan wanted the strings to be of different lengths so that it can reach different distances and also thought that winding them back would be easier.

A kind man, Billy did not show any dissent and went ahead in making all change requests demanded by Ryan. But still the project was a failure as the strings with varying lengths resulted in innumerable knots while fishing and made winding them back an impossible task.

Complicated to *impossible* would sound like a relationship getting worse. But they did manage to turn it around.

They remodelled the same project, and that became their first success. To snatch victory, they designed a large elongated spear with small holes. Each hole housed a hook connected to the main string. They had a mechanical lever in the fishing rod which, when pulled, triggered the hooks to eject simultaneously from their housing and catch hold of the fishes close to the holes in a flash. It became very popular, and later they added more features like electronic display to show the possible number of catches by detecting the fishes in proximity to the hook holes.

There was no looking back for Ryan and Billy from there. They soon were hailed as great innovators and considered among the elite people in that coastal city of Blueshells.

Still, that was not a good enough reason to keep them clinging to each other forever. They did break up at the peak of their achievement to prove who was more valuable to the other. Ryan was highly confident that his success story would continue as he was the one who held the spark. He hired a brilliant graduate to fit into the role of Billy. The youngster was not as committed as Billy was, according to Ryan. But then, who could work without an eye on the clock except for the homeless Billy? Lack of patience drove Ryan to get rid of the kid in no time, and he put himself into hiatus.

Billy had his own lessons learnt. And it was only a matter of time that they would get back together. Their rejoining was facilitated by Rosy at the mayor's birthday bash; that had been the only other time Ryan had ever graced the event with his presence. It was quite ironic to unite two unsociable personalities at the city's most sociable event. It had happened almost six years earlier.

After their reunion, the e-netcatcher was their major contribution to the world of fishing.

After Billy's demise at the age of forty-three, owing to lung cancer caused by his smoking habit, Ryan was well aware that he would not be able to find someone as good as Billy. He had long buried the thoughts that he could do wonders even without Billy. He always believed that the education system had deteriorated a lot and that the present generation's crop of graduates were more sophisticated and unwilling to hustle.

Sandy Wonka was definitely not going to be any exception from his beliefs. Ryan wanted to prove that right, and hence, he gave Sandy the toughest job straight away.

He directed Sandy to make a device that would be used in house boats to catch the fishes and detect their deliciousness and also clean and apply seasonings and spices and fry and present to the guests with a completely cooked fish ready to be eaten.

Sandy did not back off even though she felt it was a big assignment to start with. She started putting in her best efforts while Merjella was not very pleased at the way Ryan was handling her. She was unwilling to intervene in the early stage. But with the way Sandy Wonka expended her energy into the job assigned, she managed to win the heart of Merjella.

On the contrary, Ryan started to behave indifferently. He showed no interest in seeing the progress in her work. Rather, he spent time blaming the younger generation and their shallow knowledge, annoying everyone at home.

He would show no respect when Sandy would come up with questions about the requirements.

He would give a damning look at her and mutter, 'I gave you all requirements that are needed. I only want to see a working model made. Till then, instead of thinking about asking me questions, you better think about how to finish your job. I have given you such an easy work so you won't feel the pressure of working here.' After saying that, he would continue pursuing his job of tirelessly torturing his television set with able assistance from the remote control.

Merjella soon lost her patience. She directed Sandy to stop the work and asked her to inform Ryan that the work was over. Sandy Wonka followed exactly what Merjella instructed her to do. Ryan was a little surprised at the speed with which the project was done, and yet he desisted from seeing it.

He was presented with a new device. In order to test it, they brought the device near the big fish tank in his hall. The huge fish tank was his testing ground. They inserted the wide end of the hose of the newly made device, which will attract fishes and catch them. They plugged the device on to the power cord nearby.

Everything was set up, and they were all eager to see the new device functioning. When Ryan was about to switch the device on, Merjella made him into a small-sized fish, the Ryanfish, like she had before. She gave him gills and fins too and put him into the tank.

Catchmore was shocked, and he shivered inside the tank. He kept himself away from the machine. He used his limbs to climb the walls of the tank, but it was so slippery for him to get any hold. Merjella lifted him up and held him hanging from her fingers.

'You wanted to test the machine. Why are you trying to come out?' she questioned.

'Let me out. I want to test from outside!' he screamed.

'No. You should check the machine's functioning from inside. Check if it catches the fishes properly, and check if the delimeter and its piercing needle are working fine. And also check if the machine mixes seasoning and spices in proportion and if it spreads them on you uniformly. Check also if the frying section fries you completely. We are here outside to check if you are tasty enough,' Merjella explained her idea of testing.

'No no no!' pleaded Ryan with his hands held together.

'We don't need these machines, Mr Catchmore. Time is running out. We are at war. We need to build new weapons that can be used by fishes. We need to train them.'

'*You* need! Not *we*!' Ryan muttered low to himself.

'I think I heard something,' warned Merjella.

'Okay! Okay! We shall do that!' Ryan caved in.

Merjella restored him. She wanted Ryan and Sandy to work together in devising innovative means of warfare. She was very particular in creating weapons that would not be hazardous to the environment. Sandy, rooting from Pynto, had the educational background while stressing on green warfare and was considered a big asset. They were given strict orders to keep away chemicals, oil products, and radiation from the sea. That clearly meant that only spears, swords, and arrows would be employed, but their job was to implement necessary advancements in those conventional weapons.

Sandy slowly became a trusted friend of Merjella. Judging the need of the hour, she put the work at the top end of her priorities. As the job intensified, she hardly went back to her home. Ryan's garage became her home too.

13

TERROR STRIKE

One morning, even before dawn, Sandy was already busy at work. Ryan was still warming up the couch, snoring. The couch became his permanent bed as his room was taken over by Miss Wonka.

Merjella was in the kitchen, making coffee for everyone at home. Qwerty was sleeping in her beautifully decorated jar house. Despite Merjella advising her to learn to sleep with good air, Qwerty preferred her jar house filled with water. She always felt sleeping in the water gave her the satisfaction of a good sleep.

As the coffee was ready, Merjella brought the kettle and glasses to the hall and sat in front of the television. Sandy joined her at the table. Merjella poured coffee into two cups as Ryan was still sleeping. With a coffee cup in her left hand, Merjella picked up the remote control of the television and switched it on.

As she flipped through the channels, there was a news flash about a train accident that occurred in a bizarre fashion near a city called Toopa. Merjella raised the volume to listen to the details of the incident. That woke Ryan up, and he started complaining about the noise. The news claimed that almost six hundred people lost their lives in that terrible accident involving two trains speeding in opposite directions and followed by a huge explosion.

Soon the news channels were in contest to run the best possible visuals of that tragic incident. One channel captured visuals of a group of monkeys on the side of the accident area. They were seen smiling at the corpses. It was a rather strange sight for anyone.

Ryan was finally up from his sleep and had his cup of coffee.

'Don't understand what the terrorists are gaining by killing these innocents,' said Merjella.

'Innocents? Who?' Ryan questioned back.

'What's wrong with you, Ryan? Wake up properly!' Merjella shook his shoulder.

'No, I mean nobody is innocent. Everybody is working for something or someone.'

'Then how do you intend to call the common people?'

'Certainly not innocents! Why are they innocents?'

'They are innocents because they don't do deliberate killings and they are not licenced to. They would not resort to taking others' lives even if their lives were endangered.'

'So you call them innocents because of their non-aggressive stance?'

'Aggressive or non-aggressive! They don't know how to harm. They don't know how to kill. They don't play out of the law. They stick to values. They are innocents no matter what you call them. And they need to be protected.'

'Maybe they are innocents because they are committed to a system without their own concern or knowledge. Don't you think that by adhering to the rules and regulations of the system, they are asserting their belief in the system? By doing so, they are strengthening the system, and they become the core value of the system. For someone who is outside the system, attacking these innocents will produce results straight away. The system will collapse easily. That's what the terrorists want. Collapse the system and take over. Killing a well-trained soldier is tougher than getting rid of a simple man, whom the soldier had vowed to protect.' Ryan came up with his analysis.

'Still they are innocents. They are the ones that don't harm anyone, and such lives should never be harmed.'

'But they toil for the system. They represent the system that strives for harmony. They work for it, and by default, they are the soldiers of the system. They cannot be called innocents as they are very much a part of it. Innocents are those who sit idly and contribute nothing to the system. They are not loyal to anything. They keep complaining no matter who is controlling the system and what is going on in the system. They only do the talking but seldom show any action.'

'Do you know what?' said Merjella.

'What?'

'You are doing exactly that. Doing the talking and not acting. You are the only one who can be called an innocent in the way you describe innocence!'

'I just meant to say that the men who work for the system should not bother about their lives. They just have to be brave.'

While they were still in the middle of the conversation, Merjella got up and slipped out of the place. Qwerty followed her too. Neither Sandy nor Ryan noticed their absence as they were both glued to the loud television screen.

At Toopa, among the ruins, there were several teams of volunteers offering their hands to clean up the place. They were literally cleaning up the place as there were not much survivors from that accident. Being in close proximity to the forest, the place was already circled by eagles and wild dogs. Some helping hands took the job of chasing them off the scene. Strangely, there were two beautiful peacocks—one in a normal size and the other very small but with fully grown feathers. They both spread their feathers and danced for a few minutes, catching the attention of the people around. The crowd was first surprised by the smiling monkeys in the area and now the dancing peacocks.

The big peacock looked at the place closely and slowly half-closed her eyelids. Soon the place started to travel back in time. The eagles were flying back. The wild dogs were dispersing backwards into the jungle they came from. The volunteers were walking backwards. And the monkeys went hiding over the nearby trees. And the two huge trains that were in pieces after the collision stood up majestically and pulled themselves back into those strong steel tracks.

Merjella, the peacock, did not stop the turning back of time. She went ahead to see what happened to the place before the accident. She put all her might into going further back in time. To her shock, the two separate tracks were converged at that point and had some explosives tied to it. When she further pulled back time, the culprits were identified to be the smiling monkeys. As the time reversed, they were seen untying the explosives and restoring back the two tracks that ran into one.

The reversal of time came to a halt, and both peacocks took a clean look at the place. They flew to nearby signal posts on either side of the accident area and set them to be lit red permanently. They sat on the nearby olive tree and kept watch on the place. A gang of five monkeys arrived, carrying heavy tools and some explosives. They were all well built and of the same sizes—as if they were all cloned.

As the monkeys started to dismantle the railway tracks, they heard the roar of a tiger. The scared monkeys turned to see it. There stood a little black cat with green eyes. The cat purred at them. One of the monkeys took the responsibility of chasing the cat while the others continued with the job. As the monkey came chasing her, the cat (Qwerty) ran towards a tree. Once the monkey reached the tree, a pink tiger pounced on him and tore him into pieces. The helpless monkey died.

The other monkeys got alerted and started throwing explosives at the tiger. She avoided the bombs thrown at her and started advancing towards the monkeys in the track.

The sound of the explosives brought panicked people from nearby areas into that spot. They witnessed something that they could hardly believe—four monkeys, with explosives in their hands, attacking a pink tiger. The crowd stood a little away, fearing the explosives, but did not fail to inform the local police of the incident.

As the media and police poured in, the monkeys were still standing in the centre of the rail track with their hands held together, and each one was facing a different direction. The tiger was at a safe distance, keeping a constant eye on the monkeys. The cat was standing alongside the wild cat. A stalemate was going on between them. The monkeys were left with little ammunition as they initially wasted much, throwing them at random. They had to use the remaining ones effectively; otherwise, they would be torn apart.

At some distance, the forest rangers, with their rifles, were taking aim at all the animals, including the tiger. As the time passed by, the trains from both directions reached there, but they were stalled by the vigilant guards.

The stalemate would end any time soon. The eyes of the monkeys, the eyes of the tigers, and the eyes of the forest rangers were all defying the urge to blink.

In a flash, the monkeys scattered and attacked in all directions, but three were shot dead by the shooters. The only monkey that managed to escape rushed towards one of the trains and took a heave to throw the explosives but was grabbed by the tiger at the right time. Still the explosives went off, damaging the engine of the train and also injuring the tiger. Her front left leg got hurt and started to bleed. With that, she jumped into the bushes and disappeared. The cat followed her too.

Back at Ryan's place, Ryan and Sandy were still glued to the television set. Merjella and Qwerty entered through the main door with her left hand injured and bleeding.

'Where were you, Merjella? Do you know what's making news today?' asked Ryan without noticing her hands.

'What is it, Ryan?' Merjella asked back. She rushed to the garage where he had a first-aid kit.

'You will not believe this—a pink tiger with black stripes. And there was a fight between the tiger and monkeys in the middle of a railway track. It seems the monkeys have stolen explosives from somewhere, and they were attacking the tiger madly.'

Merjella applied medicine to the injury and had that bandaged. She then went to the hall to watch the news. It was then that Ryan saw her hands.

'What happened to your hands, Merjella?'

'Nothing, Ryan. A street dog attacked me. Just some bruises. Nothing to worry about.'

'You don't need such a dressing for simple bruises, Merjella. Something's wrong. Moreover, dog bites are dangerous. You need to have an anti-rabies injection.'

'Come, Merjella. My dad will help.' Sandy offered to help.

'It is okay, Sandy. I've taken precautions. I'll be all right.' She then requested Sandy to make coffee for her. Sandy Wonka obliged and went to the kitchen.

'They say that the pink tiger saved many lives. That's so stupid,' commented Ryan on the news.

'Why would that sound stupid, Ryan? The monkeys had explosives, and they were there to attack the people. If not for the tiger, hundreds of lives would have been compromised, right?'

'No, Merjella. The human lives were subjected to risk because of that tiger. If I had been in charge of the situation, I would've ordered the shooting of the tiger first.'

'Thank God, you weren't in charge! Why would you think the tiger was responsible for the lives being in danger?'

'Both the tiger and the monkeys should have come from the nearby forest. There isn't any doubt about that. My guess is that the tiger kept hunting the monkeys, and the monkeys were fast losing their species. They then plotted to attack the tiger, and hence, they must have stolen the explosives. If we had shot the tiger dead, they would've returned back to the forest happily.'

'You are a genius, Ryan. But if the fight was between the tiger and the monkeys, why would the monkey throw explosives at the train? And why did the tiger risk her life to stop the explosives directed at the train?'

Sandy came back with coffee, and it was served to all of them.

Taking a sip of coffee, Ryan said, 'Well, the tiger just attacked the monkey. It didn't try to save anyone.'

'Why do you refuse to believe something that is universally accepted?'

'Why would you believe something blindly just because everyone says so?' Ryan questioned back.

'You are right, Ryan. The tiger should have been killed, and it would've saved us some valuable time from this argument.' After saying that, Merjella picked up the remote control and pushed the power switch on the remote. She then left for her room to have a rest.

14

TRAINING FISHES

Merjella knew that building an army of fishes would be a huge task. The process was going to involve enrolment of the right species of fishes, and moreover, they had to be trained and motivated for the purpose.

Under the supervision of Merjella, Ryan Catchmore and Sandy Wonka developed strategies for the 'green' warfare under the sea. They strictly built weapons and machines that would do no harm to the environment. Working against time, they filled the gallery with effectively designed and built arms and ammunitions.

After careful study of several species of fishes and their characteristics, they shortlisted for training three varieties of fishes for military purposes and two other species for construction and livelihood purposes. Archerfish, flying fish, and mantis shrimp were the ones preferred for the martial cause.

The powerful mantis shrimps were an obvious choice to strengthen the army. They were considered a valuable addition to the army as they could smash the opponents with their extraordinary power. They were the perfect choice to attack in close ranges.

Archerfish, which had a laterally compressed body with protractile mouths, were natural fighters. They were thought to be effective in attacking from a distance as they had the ability to shoot water jets at a striking force on the enemies with their mouths. They did that with great precision, and that quality made them an easy choice for organizing the archery unit.

The flying fish were chosen for their ability to leap out of the water and take flight and glide on air. As they could traverse both water and air, they were seen as a positive addition on both the defensive and offensive fronts. Their defences were considered strong as they can escape easily by taking a leap out of the water when they come under attack. Similarly, when they are in attacking mode, they had the advantage of sighting the enemy in advance as they glide through the air. Additionally, they could be employed to carry missiles through water and air, thereby taking the war into the enemy territories with much ease.

Apart from those species, they also decided on zebra fish for spying purposes as they were very much identical with the tiger fish that formed the primary army for the Chironers.

The ribbonfish were chosen to serve as the security guards. The seismic sensitivity of the ribbonfish was dependable in identifying threats in the vicinity. Merjella wanted the ribbonfish trained to alert the guards whenever any danger was detected.

Gurnards and garfish were chosen for the construction of the city while damselfish were for vegetation purposes.

Qwerty and Bingo were busy addressing the fish folk and bringing them to one fold. They visited every colony of fishes and identified the strong ones among those species. They talked to the families about the honour of working with the army and brought them to the army camp, from where they were absorbed using the e-netcatcher.

The new e-netcatcher was modified a little to pick up fishes based on power and stamina factors. Instead of the delimeter, they installed a power gauge that would measure the strength of the fishes. Millions of fishes were brought into Catchmore's place, and they were given regular drills in different aquarium halls in order to keep them fit.

The fishes were ordered into several columns. They were interviewed, and smarter ones were spotted to lead regiments. Qwerty took the responsibility of communicating with the new soldiers in the initial stage. The fish armies were divided into various regiments, and colonels were appointed. Proper hierarchy was established, and discipline was imparted among the soldiers.

Despite their efforts going on in full swing, Merjella was not happy with the progress. She felt something was missing in the training. Her intuition was warning her about something which she could not find out. She was also disturbed by thoughts of programmed animals being used against mankind. The incident with the monkeys attacking the trains was still occupying her head. She could hardly relax.

Merjella asked Ryan and Sandy to arrange for a war rehearsal. The next morning, a huge aquarium was readied, with corals and other structures arranged. Sandy Wonka placed dummy figures concealed in those artificial reefs. Thousands of trained fishes were brought to the tank. Merjella entered the tank too, along with Qwerty, Ryan, and Sandy.

Qwerty gave instructions to the soldiers comprising of archerfish, flying fish, and mantis shrimps. She wanted them to destroy the enemy fish figures that were marked with red tags. The soldiers were informed that they have to collect the tags, and the regiment that collects the maximum number of tags would be rewarded. There were also a few green figures that should not be attacked.

All four of them stayed back to witness the performance of the army. Qwerty beat the drums randomly signalling the start of the contest. The fierce fight started.

Archerfish started shooting from a distance while mantis shrimps neared the enemy targets and knocked them down aggressively. The flying fish were able to spot hidden targets with ease, and the whole process started off well. Qwerty looked a proud master. Ryan and Sandy were happy too while Merjella was still carefully watching.

Suddenly, there was chaos, and the army started to attack ruthlessly within. Soon it went out of control, and many fish collapsed. Qwerty gave a long drum beat, signalling everyone to stop and come to order. Even as the fish obediently came to a halt, a few soldiers kept picking up the red tags spread all over. Ryan and Sandy pulled out the injured fishes and gave them the necessary medical attention.

Merjella grabbed the conical megaphone and addressed the army, 'We have failed, my friends. We have failed miserably.' The army of fishes put their heads down, listening to her.

Merjella looked at a captain and asked, 'What was the need for attacking our own people?'

The captain replied politely that they were robbed of the red tags that their team deserved. Immediately, other captains protested, saying that their tags were taken away too and that they deserved more. As the arguments among the fishes started, Merjella raised her arms to calm them down.

'The aim of this program is to defeat the enemies. That is our primary goal. Collecting tags is in fact not an essential thing. It is just a diversion. One who is determined to win will focus on winning rather than on the rewards that come with it. Rewards without wins are meaningless while wins with no rewards will still earn you honour. We are here to build a nation for us. And we all should pledge for a strong nation.' Merjella looked into the eyes of the fishes. They were all bright and illumed.

A soldier raised her fin, seeking permission to talk.

Merjella signalled for her to go ahead.

'What is a nation? Why do we need one?' the soldier posed.

Many fishes nodded as if that was their question too.

'Well, a nation will be our identity, our pride, our belief, and the one that will unite us, harmonize us, and drive us to live better and prosper further. Every morning, we wake up to fears of being attacked or killed by a stronger species. Fearing this, we either live in hiding or move constantly to evade our enemies. All through our lives, we will be spending our time and energy in just being alert and chasing our food. And when we die, our fish world will remain exactly the same as when we were born. That also puts our next generations into the same things we have been through. By building a nation, we will have an opportunity to give a prominent lead to our offspring. With security and other needs taken care of, we can spend our time thinking of ways to improve our lives—lives of ease that prolong our existence. The sacrifices we make today will only yield results tomorrow—to our successors. But our names will be etched in history as the pillar stones of the great nation we have built together.'

The army vibrated with so much positivity upon listening to her speech. They vibrated in unison. The water was filled with good resonance.

'What is our nation called?' questioned General Mike, an archerfish who led Regiment 12.

'Seasorg,' replied Ryan Catchmore.

'Seasorg, the Heaven in the Sea,' reiterated Merjella.

'Long live Seasorg!' chanted the fishes valiantly.

15

SEASORG

Seasorg was strategically located with both security and resources in mind. The area was handpicked by Ryan with his wide knowledge of the sea, and it was authorized by Merjella. Her main concern remained the safety of fellow fishes.

Bingo was crowned as the first president of Seasorg. He was given able ministers to assist him. Merjella had high confidence in Bingo's abilities to handle things. She always felt he was a smart one.

The layout for Seasorg was created by Ryan and handed over to garfish and gurnards to complete the construction work. They also planned fortified walls and nets around the city. Gurnards were used to mobilize the resources necessary for building purposes. They were able to walk through the seabed and were efficient in carrying materials. Garfishes were skilled in placing and positioning the rocks and binding them strongly.

Schools, barracks, and hospitals were the first priority. There were plans to establish banks, refineries, markets, fuel stations, workshops, and underwater telecom towers in the future.

Even before the construction work started, they erected a main entrance arch for the city. The arch was garrisoned with two strong patrols of mantis shrimps carrying strong spears. Ribbonfish were employed to foresee any untoward incidents that could harm the city. Their ability to pick up even the slightest vibrations was banked on to detect impending threats. They were made to patrol the borders with constant eyes and ears. Their job was to convey alarms as soon as they felt movement near the borders, and the special force would act immediately to assess the danger level. They were all well connected with the mobile telephony service.

Schools were established to provide essential knowledge to the fishes. Elderly fishes with vast knowledge were recruited as teachers. Apart from imparting knowledge, they concentrated on imparting discipline on to the younger generations.

Citizens were enrolled at a separate counter. They were issued identity medals and provided with a mobile, a place to stay, and a thousand stellars each. Stellar was the currency, and they were made of waterproof paper and were printed and distributed by Ryan himself.

The fishes initially found it hard to understand the concept of currency, and they tended to overspend. Later, the central bank intervened and regularized the prices of all commodities. They also conducted street meetings to educate the folks about the importance of stellars and that they had to earn more and more stellars to lead a cosy life.

'Hello! Am I talking to Quela?' A fish called up another over the mobile.

'Yes, right! Who are you?'

'I am Kryzyn! Do you remember me, Quela?'

'Hey, Kryzyn. How are you? How could I forget you?'

'I'm doing good, Quela. How are you and your folks?'

'All good, Kryzyn. How did you get my number?'

'I got it from the citizens' register. I had to pay ten stellars for that.'

'Oh, sweet!'

'Tell me something, dear!'

'No! Nothing! You say something!'

'Mmmm . . . Have you had your dinner?'

'Yes. You?'

'Yes. Just now.'

'Then?'

'Then nothing! You say something!'

'Nothing, you say something!'

This was a common conversation that could be overheard on the mobile networks.

Damselfish were allotted lands to practice agriculture, and research stations were established as well. Bingo was overseeing all these activities. He made it a habit to check all those enrolled at the end of each day. He was on top of everything. He was polite and heeded to everyone's demands.

One day, before going to sleep, Bingo ordered for the immigration list for that day as usual, and he was presented with it. He went through the list very carefully.

Matio? Circa? Bingo read to himself. 'Take me to the place where they are put up,' Bingo ordered his staff.

In no time, his vehicle was ready to take him. The president's vehicle was a shell with a very hard material that cannot be broken open. Inside the shell, there was a well-cushioned seat, and the water inside was conditioned at a temperature that can be controlled. There was enough food stored inside in case of emergencies. The shell was chained to a stand-alone motor with a steering wheel, which only an A-grade guard was authorized to drive. The vehicle was allowed to take off only when a minimum of six guards on their own wheels followed it.

The key to the shell would be at the hands of the president only. He could open the shell only after receiving a signal from all six guards. In case of emergencies or any attacks while in transit, the guards were ordered to cut down the chain of the shell, and the shell would be deposited at the bottom. The shell was loaded with things to help hold the president for about two months. A duplicate key was in the parliament, which would need authorization from three ministers and can only be used to open the shell in the presence of strong security of at least a hundred soldiers around. The shell was designed to withstand any calamities, including powerful bombs and strong earthquakes.

The shell had a sensor too, which would help Ryan locate that when lost. And he too possessed a key for the shell. He also knew other ways to open the shell.

With guards around, Bingo started his journey. He was taken to where Matio was placed. As Bingo got down, his guards took position. They trained their guns at the door of Matio's home. Bingo looked at that place for a moment. One of his soldiers went ahead and knocked on the door. It was Matio who came answering the door. He was an elderly starfish dark green in colour. Circa was seen behind him. Bingo's eyes widened, and tears started to flow from his eyes.

'Papa! Mama!' He went straight to them and hugged them.

'We are so proud of you, my son,' said Matio.

'When you left the home, we were very sad. We are sorry, Bingo, for the way we have treated you,' said Circa.

'No, Mama. Your beatings helped me to become what I am now. It was my mistake to run away from home. I am sorry, Mama, Papa!' pleaded the president.

It was quite an emotional family reunion. Bingo then took them with him to his presidential residence. They were a happy family again.

The sudden activities in that region did not fail to invite attention from the Chironers. Chiro was duly informed about the developments. There were lots of supplies blocked from reaching Zypher. Most fishes stopped supplying foods and other valuables to Zypher, and they preferred the Seasorg life.

Meanwhile, Merjella went to inspect the new city along with Qwerty, Ryan, and Sandy. They were also provided with gills and fins to survive and move easily in that deep sea.

'We were so delighted to know you have found your family back, Bingo. We wanted to come right away to see you, Mr Matio, but then we were held up,' Merjella expressed her pleasure in meeting Bingo's parents.

'We are quite happy to meet you too, Jella and Qwerty, my son's best friends!' said Matio.

'We would be pleased to meet Mimico too. But unfortunately . . .' Circa felt it was unutterable.

'Mama, we will soon save him. Don't you worry,' consoled Bingo.

They then went on to inspect the progress of Seasorg. Merjella was puzzled at the way currencies were put into use. The marketplace was dumped with clothing and fashion accessories. She was surprised to see the fishes thronging at the markets and bargaining to buy things they wanted.

'Where do they come from?' Merjella asked Bingo.

Ryan Catchmore turned to the other side as if he was seriously observing something else.

'The Department of Imports oversees that, Jella. Our Ryan gives all these accessories. He has promised more,' Bingo replied.

'Ryan!' Merjella called for his attention.

'Yes! Yes!'

'Why do you complicate their life too much? Why would you bring some stupid paper and call them stellars and sell unwanted fashion articles?'

'I am just experimenting, Merjella!'

'Experimenting with my folks? Huh . . .' After a small pause, Merjella continued, 'What will you gain from this, Ryan?'

'Nothing. Nothing really, Merjella.'

Sandy signalled something to Merjella.

'What does he take, Sandy?'

'Pearls! He takes all the pearls, Merjella.'

'Oh, oh, you issue paper currencies, you dump all unwanted articles in the name of fashion, and then you take away pearls!'

'Pearls are my fees. I have to finance myself. I am not allowed to go fishing. How do you think we could spend for all our needs?' replied Ryan in a bit of an agitated mood.

Merjella just shook her head out of disgust and moved on with the inspection. She was happy with things shaping up. She asked Sandy Wonka to plan an effective tunnel and railway service that would connect the city well. She also wanted to educate fishes on the importance of hygiene.

Merjella then called upon the Defence Department and warned them of possible attacks. She asked them to be vigilant at all hours. Then she decided to leave Qwerty in Seasorg and ordered for the same level of security as the president for her too.

'No, I want to be with you always, Jella! That's what Mimico also instructed me. Did you forget?' appealed Qwerty.

'I know, Qwerty. You are right. Mimico told you to be with me all the time. But he didn't mean "being with me" in a physical sense. You are supposed to back me up. That's what being with me means. We are going to bring more and more armed forces here, and only you can coordinate with them. Only you know the idea of the whole thing we are into.'

'Okay, Jella! But only till the war is over. After that, we are not separating on any condition.'

Jella promised and left for Blueshells with Ryan and Sandy. Immediately after assuming office, Qwerty summoned the immigration staff. They were ordered to send her a copy of enrolled citizens like they had reported to Bingo.

Once she was presented with the list, she went through it. She tried to observe it carefully, but then she tended to skip after a few minutes, and later on, she would yawn. She would lose patience and ask the officers to read the list for her. She realized she did not have enough patience, and so she ordered them to bring it to her attention if anyone named Berta registered in the city.

The next morning, the immigration office called her up and informed her that there were about sixty-seven already in that name and three more have arrived at their office that day.

Sixty-seven and three more today? Qwerty said to herself. 'Anyone with a purple tail like I have?' questioned Qwerty.

'No, madam. Not anyone we have enrolled today.'

'Fine. Just do search on all those Bertas and inform me immediately when you find a purple-tailed one. It is an emergency,' commanded Qwerty, and she hung up the call.

'What are you trying to do, Qwerty?' posed Bingo, who overheard the phone call.

'I am trying to find my brother Berta. He should be here as well.'

'Well, I wish that you will get back your family too, Qwerty!' Bingo beamed.

Meanwhile, on the border, ribbonfish reported an alert to the archerfish guards. The guards took position and stood alert. Soon, they spotted a battalion of tiger fish from Zypher. Bingo was informed of a probable attack and that they were ready.

'Strictly no loss of lives. Execute things perfectly!' Bingo told the archerfish guards.

The tiger fish gasped from a distance for some time. They tried to measure if there was any risk involved. After they were convinced, they took off at a fast pace to storm Seasorg through the arch. They held the sharp ends of their swords pointing forwards and ready to tear off anything on the way. They were coming at a ferocious pace, and as they were about to cross the gate, they all were struck by a solid body, throwing them apart. Before they could recover from the blow, they were taken as prisoners.

'This is what we call glass, friends,' a guard told one of the enemy fish. 'You should ask permission to enter.'

The tiger fish were then stripped of all their weapons and packed in a thick transparent polythene bag and hung near the arch as a display for the enemies to take note of.

The vengeance-seeking tiger fish hit the cover madly with their heads, intending to tear it open, but it was in vain. The guards had enough amusement out of that scene. The news had a positive response among the citizens, and they celebrated their might. Bingo hosted a special dinner to his high-level officials in appreciation for the work.

As the dinner was going on, Qwerty received a call.

'Madam, this is an emergency. We have spotted a purple-tailed Berta.'

'Wow! This is a great day for me! Bring him to my place. He is my brother. Treat him accordingly,' ordered Qwerty.

The immigration officials organized for an extensive program to celebrate the reunion of the siblings. They readied a well-decorated chariot and picked Berta from his home. The whole procession to the palace was led by a group of musicians and dancers. They kept the atmosphere alive and vibrant all along.

The palace was already experiencing the high-voltage party with all kinds of string instruments being played. Vibrations were all around the place. Qwerty and Bingo's families were expecting Berta eagerly at the palace, and he arrived there amidst strong celebrations.

As Berta reached them, Bingo went straight ahead and received him. He was taken into the palace.

'Wait! You are not Berta!' remarked Qwerty.

'I am Berta!' said Berta.

'But not my brother Berta.'

'Yes! Not your brother Berta!'

Everyone went silent. Everyone looked embarrassed. It was a tough call to say who was embarrassed the most—maybe Berta. He was so disappointed about the anticlimax of such a reception. He was about to leave the place when he was stopped.

'Berta!' called Qwerty.

Berta turned back and looked at Qwerty as if asking her what she wanted.

'But your purple tail—are you related to me by any means?'

'Oh, the purple tail. Mine is yellow actually. I got this purple-coloured tail polish from the market and only recently applied it. They said girls get attracted to purple. They also said you are a girl.'

Bingo could not stop laughing. And so did everyone else in the gathering.

16

MARINA AND DEIMOS

Meanwhile, on land, the world was preparing to witness the wedding of the decade—the royal wedding between the prince of Merryland and the princess of Fairina.

Though Merryland was one of the earliest democracies in the world, the monarchy managed to hold its roots. The king and the queen of Merryland not only prevailed over the surge of people's thrust into power, but more importantly, they won huge respect and love from the people. The monarchy even enjoyed active space in the political constitution of Merryland.

Even though the country shared borders with seven sovereign neighbours, it was very well protected. With all her perimeter sealed tightly, Merryland enjoyed an intruder-proof terrain, ensuring peace and cover for the citizens. Fairina was the country that shared the largest portion of Merryland's lengthy borderline. It was still under the reign of King Wilson VII. His only granddaughter, Princess Alyssa, was engaged to Prince Stevens of Merryland.

The palace of Merryland was prepared majestically to host the grand wedding ceremony. With this being a high-profile event, the security preparations were on top of everything.

The media all over the world went agog over the marriage and reported tirelessly about every advancement in the program.

'Why all this hype?' wondered Ryan upon skimming over the morning newspaper.

'Why not? Prince Charming and Princess Grace are getting married. Don't you find that amazing?' said Merjella.

'But this is the age of democracy. Where is the place for kings and queens?'

'Oh, Ryan, you stingy politician! Why not think generously? Just imagine the lives of kings, queens, princes, princesses. That's so spectacular. You have everyone at your service. The feeling of a princess—I just love that. And getting married to a prince—wow! I call that a perfect wedding, Ryan. Even if you are not a princess, it makes you feel like one,' Merjella confessed.

'I wish to have been born a prince too! Maybe I won't be complaining about anything if I am the king.'

'Maybe you will still be querulous about the plight of the haves, Ryan.'

'Maybe not,' Ryan protested.

'Why not? I was thinking you love complaining. It seems you complain even though you don't like complaining.'

'Who in this world would love complaining?'

'But why in this world would someone do something that they don't like? Let alone something that is not liked by others as well,' Merjella questioned back.

Ryan remained silent, indicating that he had no answer for that. He then continued, 'This wedding is going to attract unwanted incidents.'

'No. Nothing bad will happen.'

'How are you so sure, Merjella?'

'Because I am going to be there, Ryan. If you want, you can come with me,' Merjella extended the invitation to Catchmore, and he refused without giving it a thought, which was not unexpected of him.

The wedding attracted a huge crowd from all over the world because of the political importance it carried. For more than three decades, Merryland and Fairina had rivalled each other at every possible level. The fierce exchanges of fire at the frontier between both nations should still be nursing the memories of the soldiers, and the wedding brought them together at the disposal of the kings taking charge of the security services.

Merjella, dressed in an elegant full-skirted backless yellow gown, appeared second only to the bride. The real princess was wearing a long white strapless gown tied tightly with laces in the back. The top of the gown was designed like a butterfly to indicate the beautiful symmetry of her chest. There were indeed small antennae-like patterns to confirm the butterfly design. The huge crowd that gathered outside the Grand Church to witness the wedding did not have a good reason to look out for the second best gracing the occasion. Very few invitees were allowed inside, and that only included top politicians and aristocrats from around the world. Everyone in the crowd was scrambling to catch a glimpse of the young royal couple.

The crowd, the bride, the bridegroom, the ministers, the VIPs, the constant drumbeats, and the prevailing festive mood did not fail to invoke the memories of Marina's own marriage. Her wedding was arranged at the famous St Anne Church in Pynto, where hundreds of scientists and politicians marked the event with their presence to celebrate with the couple. The biggest difference between the two marriages was that Marina's did not feature a huge public crowd like the princess's. Moreover, both Marina's and Deimos's parents had been absent. Marina's were no more while Deimos's were not in talking terms with him.

Marina and Deimos were considered to be the most promising young scientists of the era. And hence the occasion was treated with tremendous significance among the science enthusiasts. Most believed there were going to be bigger advancements due to that marriage, and hence most of the greetings and wishes were made along that line.

'May the world be blessed with a greater leap in science with your marriage!'

'May the good Lord shower you with power to enlighten the future of this world!'

Their choice for their honeymoon, Eyecandy, was not a big surprise. But because of Deimos's busy schedule, they kept postponing their honeymoon trip. Deimos worked on a big project for his boss, whose identity Deimos never let out because of confidentiality terms, while Marina was content in supporting her husband by being at home.

Staying back at home after the marriage was Marina's own decision as she wanted to make it easy to find time together with Deimos. She foresaw that both of them indulging in their own passions would curtail every possibility of their time together. Despite her calculated moves, the marriage still went awry. Their initial days as man and wife were terrible, and it only worsened with time.

Marina felt a big change in Deimos, with their relationship transforming from lovers to spouses. When they were lovers, Deimos's attention on her was way too much. She had it tough finding time for herself and for him simultaneously. She imagined life to be fairytale-like after marriage. She thought Deimos's top priority would be her at any instant. That was the reason she had put him on top of her priorities and ahead of her own dreams.

Before marriage, she was being constantly disturbed by both him and thoughts of him. But after marriage, only the thoughts of him remained disturbing her; Deimos was nowhere in the picture. That could quite be her delusion because she was busy with her own things before they tied the knot. Since she freed herself from all her commitments for the sake of marriage, she was mostly idling and looking for more attention from her beloved Deimos. On the other hand, Deimos got busy day after day. He did spend considerable time with Marina, but that was all for their new project called *pro-dog*. Apart from that, they did not make valuable time for their personal selves. Marina at times thought that Deimos married her for her value as a scientist and nothing more than that. Yet she was happy that there was at least something that kept their marriage alive and going. She always had that hope lingering in her heart that the good days were yet to arrive.

Slowly, their differences got bigger and bigger. There were arguments over simple and silly things. On some days, the casual conversations between them grew into deeper disputes. Their emotional distance did not hinder her from getting pregnant. Deimos, who was immersed in his work, did not find it easy to handle too. He felt undue pressure out of the marriage, and he kept distancing himself from Marina. His priority shifted clearly in favour of his dreams. He always had the feeling that he was a little short of becoming famous and that a little more push would get him there comfortably. Every time he gave a little push, it added up to the numerous little pushes he already gave, and unbeknownst to himself, he was exerting a huge pressure on himself.

Marina tried to bring that to his attention, but it was in vain. New disputes surfaced when it was discovered that Marina was pregnant. How to bring up the child was their topic, and it always took them to severe altercations. Deimos felt Marina was more authoritative and trying to enforce herself on him, to which he always resisted. Even Marina felt the same way, and as time passed by, she started to go soft on things. She was worried about the baby she was carrying too, and hence, she avoided emotional outbursts for the sake of her offspring.

Her new relaxed approach brought positive changes. Marina could feel Deimos getting back to her. He started spending time with her. He cared for their unborn baby. As the delivery date neared, he arranged to move her to his own workplace, which had a hospital with a maternity ward. Marina could not remember a happier moment before in her entire life.

But her happiness did not last long. When the baby was delivered, Marina fell unconscious, and she could feebly hear the attendants running around on an emergency. The baby, who failed to start breathing, was rushed to the intensive care unit. When Marina came to consciousness a few hours later, Deimos was on her side. Marina looked around to spot the cradle to see her baby.

'You are not lucky, Marina,' Deimos uttered with tremendous pain in his heart. He then consoled the weeping Marina.

Marina was extremely sad remembering the incident.

17

MIMICO KILLED

Jello Jail in Zypher was a dark room built of stones with a grilled opening on just one wall; it was guarded round the clock by the watchful eyes of the swordfish. The malojels built the prison specially to lock down octopuses.

It was usually a gloomy place with either silence or whimpers filling the place. But ever since Mimico was added as an inmate, the Jello Jail acquired some life. The octopuses always gathered around him to learn stories about Jella and her mates.

'She is a princess—very beautiful! Her arms are long and soft. Her transparent body radiates a beautiful pinkish shade, which is a great delight to watch. She is gracious to every being just like our great Emperor Tarjo was.' Mimico used to repeat those descriptions tons of times every day, and the octopuses loved to hear the routine. The very utterance of the name Tarjo would bring an awed expression to the octopuses. Jella also managed to receive equal reception from the inmates.

And every day they never forgot to ask Mimico, 'Will Jella come and save us?'

And Mimico was never tired of replying, 'Yes! She will!'

To keep the hopes high in the jail, Mimico invented various stories depicting the bravery of Jella. One day it would be about how she fought a dozen sharks to rescue her friends, and the next day it would be the story of her fighting the hungry whales.

'Who are her friends, Mimico?'

'Bingo and Qwerty. Bingo is from a family of starfish. He has very expressive large eyes for a starfish, green-coloured. He is very strong. Qwerty is a tiny yellow fish with a long purple tail. She is a trained fighter too—very sincere and intelligent. Right now she should be hatching plans to break into Zypher and take us to freedom,' Mimico said amidst the enthusiastic octopuses.

Meanwhile, Qwerty was having dinner with Berta in a restaurant in Seasorg.

'Thanks for making my day special, Qwerty!' Berta looked enthusiastic. He held Qwerty's pectoral fin and kissed it.

'You are so sweet, Berta. I wish we can meet often,' said the love-struck Qwerty.

'I love you, Qwerty,' Berta confessed, and his eyes were madly following Qwerty's.

'Me too!'

When Qwerty came out of the restaurant, she was attacked brutally. She was clueless about who was attacking, but the onlookers chased the assailants away and saved her. Her fins were injured, and blood oozed out. She was rushed to the hospital. Bingo was furious about the incident and ordered for an enquiry.

They found out that Qwerty made a secret visit to the restaurant and that she did not want her guards to tail her. And it was the orange-tailed rivals of her family that attacked her.

When she was at the hospital, most of her well-wishers made their visit. Berta was with her all the time. Jella visited her too and showed her angst about her carelessness. She then instructed Qwerty strictly to use the security services and adhere to the rules.

The surprise visitor for Qwerty was her brother Berta. It was an emotional but subtle reunion. Her brother Berta expressed his craving for revenge at orangulars, their orange-tailed cousins.

'What next?' questioned Qwerty.

'What?' Berta asked back with surprise.

'What are we going to do after taking revenge?'

'We will live happily. We will be at peace,' said Berta.

'We have been taking revenge after revenge, brother. But we were neither happy nor at peace,' spoke Qwerty.

'But then we will be taken for granted, Qwerty, if we don't strike back,' explained Berta.

'Brother! Revenge is never a solution. Every act of revenge may look like an end, but it always marks a beginning. Nobody can settle the score with revenge as nothing gets settled. I ran away from home out of fear. We lost our mother. We lost our father. We lost our family for nothing. It is time we fight for a cause. Let's fight for a safe Seasorg. Let's fight for pride. Let's fight for integrity. Let's fight for a place in history' were the words from the visibly emotional Qwerty. She sure did not want to lose her brother for a fight that was not worth anything.

Her brother Berta was moved, and he stood close to his sister.

At the court of Chiro in Zypher, the orange-tailed Stroba was bargaining with the information he got about Seasorg.

'We want your help to wipe out the purpulars,' demanded Stroba.

'Purpulars?'

'Yes, the ones with those ugly purple tails,' Stroba said, wagging his tail.

'Why do you want to destroy them?'

'They are ugly. Purple is ugly. We just hate them.'

'You want to kill them just because they are ugly?'

'Yes, exactly. Ugly creatures. Shame to our community.'

'Well! What information do you have about Seasorg to trade with us?'

'Bingo and Qwerty!'

'That we are aware of, dimwit,' said Chiro, and he ordered the Chironers, 'Get rid of this ugly orange-tailed—'

'Orangular,' said Stroba.

As the Chironers moved forwards to get hold of Stroba, he stuttered, 'Wait, wait! I have something you don't know.'

'What's that?' asked Chiro in a stern voice.

'Bingo is not the king of Seasorg. Jella—it is Jella who rules Seasorg. I suppose you wouldn't be knowing that,' revealed Stroba.

'Jella? Is she an octopus?'

'I am afraid not. She is more than that, my lord. She is a jellopus.'

Chiro's innumerable arms trembled out of fear on hearing that. He lost his nerves. He wasted no time to kill Stroba with a sting. He then ordered all the prisoners to be brought immediately to the Seasquare.

Soon, the whole of Zypher assembled at the Seasquare. The prisoners were brought with their arms bound tightly.

Mimico too was brought with his arms held tightly by four jellyfish to the centre of the Seasquare, where Chiro was standing.

'Who is Bingo?' Chiro started his enquiry.

'Which Bingo?' Mimico questioned back.

'Mmmm . . . I don't think you remember him. But he remembers you very well, it seems. He wants you and four others of your choice to be released in exchange for Chironers captured by him.'

The prisoners were all agog on hearing that.

'He was right. Bingo is very powerful,' said an octopus to another.

Mimico was delighted to hear that.

'Who do you want to go along with you?' asked Chiro.

'Carmello, Zaquella, Joubin . . . mmm . . . Mathello,' said Mimico. The four of them were released from claws and brought to the centre of the ring.

Chiro took a close look at them all. 'You seem to have picked all weak companions, Mimico!'

'I'm just helping the ones who need help the most, Chiro,' justified Mimico.

Chiro then came close to Mimico and looked deeply at him with one of his big eyes and murmured, 'What if they have to help you?'

Mimico stood still. Chiro ordered his associates to bring the cross. Three giant jellyfish, including Nomura, brought a cross carved from heavy rock that was denser even in the water. Chiro then ordered them to tie Mimico to the cross.

They tied two of his arms to each corner of the cross so that his body lay in the middle. Very slender and sharp twigs were used to tightly tie him so that the arms would get cut with the mounting pressure.

'Now you will tell me who Bingo is.'

'He is my friend, Chiro.'

Chiro smiled and said, 'I want more, Mimico!'

'Sure. He will give you, Chiro! He is generous unlike you,' answered Mimico wittily even as the other octopuses were watching him more sympathetically.

Chiro gave him a sucker punch, a trademark move of his, and he did not bother to withdraw his sting. He kept injecting poison into Mimico's body.

The malojels enjoyed the sight, and Aurelia was the only malojel to shed tears for Mimico. Aurelia and Mimico had been associated for long, and she was considered an angel among the malojels. She had a kind heart and broad mind, which was not usual for a malojel. She commanded certain amount of influence among the malojels. Chiro used to listen to her in most cases. It was because of her that Chiro kept the octopuses as prisoners. He had always wanted to destroy them.

Aurelia could not tolerate what was going on there. She went to the centre of the Seasquare and stood face-to-face with Chiro.

'Enough, Chiro. He is too old to bear all this,' Aurelia insisted.

'Yes, yes! You are right, angel! He is in deep pain. We should help him.' After saying this, he pulled out his tentacle, and in a flash, all his venomous tentacles spat poison into Mimico's body. Aurelia looked shocked, and so did the other octopuses.

'Now he will not feel any pain!' said Chiro, and he left the square.

Aurelia rushed to check Mimico's pulse. She declared that Mimico was dead. The octopuses felt sad and started crying. The Chironers took the prisoners inside but left the chosen four free. Aurelia helped them leave the place with Mimico's body. She ordered a unit of black angelfish to escort them to Seasorg. It was considered a symbol of state honours provided to the dead ones.

The four weak octopuses held the four corners of the cross and carried Mimico through the still waters. Joubin, with her beautiful voice, sang some songs depicting the courage and love of octopuses.

As they neared Seasorg, the news went viral. Bingo, Qwerty, the two Bertas, Matio, Circa, and all other big names in Seasorg came out to see Mimico. Jella was already in Seasorg, staying by the side of the injured Qwerty.

When the group of octopuses reached Seasorg, Bingo and the injured Qwerty helped hold the cross and brought it down. Bingo ordered the release of the captives from Zypher. They then removed the strings holding Mimico's arms and took him to the medical hall to see if any help could be done to save Mimico. The emotionally distressed Jella tried to take Mimico back through time. She was stopped by Bingo, and he reminded her that they cannot bring back the lives of the jellopuses and octopuses by time travel.

Jella still tried to pull back time, but the body of Mimico remained unchanged while all other beings moved back. Jella broke into tears. It was then that Mimico was declared dead, and a funeral was ordered. As Mimico's body was buried, Jella was consoled by Joubin, Carmello, Zaquella, and Mathello.

Then they called for an emergency cabinet meeting to discuss their future course of action. They decided to increase military power and wanted to draw a deadline to get all political prisoners from Zypher released. Questions of revenge were completely played down. They wanted to look beyond and were determined to do what was good for Seasorg.

18

THE BOSS

That Friday, the International Council was all set to celebrate their golden jubilee. It was exactly fifty years back that the council was set up just after the great economic meltdown, which was caused due to mismanagement of funds by multinational companies and banks. It was then that the countries felt the need to form a single economic zone with one currency to make it easy to track the flow.

Ever since the International Council was established, the global economy was secured and was under control. When there was something running smooth and steady, naturally there would be eagerness from some section to accelerate it. As the new generations were not exactly aware of the impacts of the economic meltdown, they started protesting against the common policy, which they felt imposed constraints that curbed their opportunity for growth. They were demonstrating in front of the International Council's headquarters located at the heart of Pynto.

They were just demonstrations and not threats. They were only demanding something from within the system. In fact, they were strengths to such organizations, injecting new dimension to the thought process of the system. The real threat would be from the ones who were going all out to destroy the system. And such threats were also flowing in.

Ever since the celebration was announced, the International Council received hundreds of threatening emails. Among them, the security department classified eleven as potential ones. They tracked down seven, and necessary actions were initiated. Among the four non-traceable threats, one was targeted at the chief secretary of the International Council, Mr Calvin Moses. And it was signed with 'The Boss'.

> Dear Calvin Moses,
>
> The golden jubilee of the International Council will mark the end of the council as the world's prime authority. The power hub is going to shift. It will be duly demonstrated by abducting you in front of a million eyes.
>
> Pitifully yours,
> The Boss

Being the chief secretary of the International Council was like being the president of the whole world. That post had that much power and popularity behind it. When someone held an office of such a stature, it was not unusual to get threats of that degree. But still the security personnel had to ensure nothing unwanted would happen on that eventful day, which would be watched by more than a billion people all over the world.

Since it was a special occasion, the world nations pledged the utmost security possible. The Grand Square, the site at which the gala was planned, was made completely intruder-proof, with surveillance cameras and motion sensors working overtime. The organizing committee was busy issuing identity cards to the authorized personnel as well as spectators. They made it mandatory for the attendees to arrive two days before the event, and the airport of the city of Pynto had been sealed since then, allowing only flights of VIPs to access the aerial route.

There were about twenty thousand security guards with the latest equipment employed. Additionally, there were 240 snipers around the Grand Square. They were working in shifts, keeping a constant eye on the happenings.

They got more alert when the ceremony was declared open by the chief secretary himself. He was addressing the gathering from a bulletproof booth with a public address system. He was voicing his concern over the new faces of terrorism.

It was then that some security guards started sighting eagles circling high above the ground. They may not be a threat to the proceedings, but then that was a strange sight in that part of the city. Soon the number of eagles grew. The security men were very concerned and wanted to take the chief secretary to safety as early as they could. It could be a sign of natural calamity to follow too. Everyone was confused. But the confusion did not last long.

The eagles flew downward in cohesion. The snipers managed to gun down a few. But by then, the eagles stormed into the glass booth, where Calvin Moses was standing, and with their strong beaks, they hooked into his dress and skin, whichever was available, and lifted him in a moment and took off together. The 'president of the world' disappeared from their sight just like that.

The crowd that witnessed the incident remained unmoving. Almost all their heads were paralyzed even from panicking. There remained an absolute silence in that jam-packed arena. Soon the crowd came to their senses and started to analyze what they had just witnessed.

The security guards were trying to gauge the level of threat that still remained. They were hustling to find a clue. A pair of helicopters already flew, tailing the eagles.

But before any breakthrough could be made, the International Council received a mail from the Boss.

To whoever is in charge,

This is the beginning of the shift of power.

Now if you may clear the Grand Square, I shall exhibit my might. I assume thirty minutes is more than enough for you to evacuate the place, paving for a grand show.

Thanking you.

Compellingly yours,
The Boss

The army went on a full-swing exercise to evacuate the place. There were chaos and panic all around.

Soon the news of the sudden disappearance of the helicopters arrived, and the whole defence crew went off guard. By clearing all the spectators from the Grand Square, the security guards were preparing the space for them to become spectators.

The Grand Square had been built about three decades ago, marking the dominance of Pynto as a great economic power in the world. The city was the natural choice to establish the International Council since almost all major financial services companies and banks had prominent presence in the city. Ever since it was built, the Grand Square remained the symbol of pride for the people of Pynto, and they were all in tears on realizing that it was to be destroyed in another few minutes. It had taken twenty-seven months to complete the whole architecture of the place that could house nearly three hundred thousand people at a time in the open ground alone. More than that, it had a huge library and a science museum.

Everyone was impatiently watching the events about to unfold.

The thirty-minute deadline was over, then another thirty minutes ran past, and another thirty minutes dried up. All they could spot was a small bird sitting on top of the flag post. The International Council's flag was flying high. It was a square teal-green flag with a saffron dot representing the globe and a white flying dove over the dot.

By that time, everyone realized that the last email was a fake threat just to gain attention or to divert attention from following the kidnapped chief secretary. The security personnel started to shift their focus to further investigation and to sketch plans to rescue Mr Moses.

It was then that the tiny blue bird spit a bomb on the flag, and it burst and burnt the flag instantly. The bird then flew away.

Soon, the third mail from the Boss reached them.

'That's all, folks!'

The security personnel then drafted a mail asking for the Boss's demands. They also picked up the dead eagles that were shot in the process and sent them for laboratory tests. They soon found out that the birds were embedded with programmable chips that were similar to the one used in the dog they captured in Kreppo several weeks back. They also resembled the chips used in programmable plants developed by Marina Jalencia. Deimos and Marina became chief suspects in the Calvin Moses kidnap case. They were convinced that the Boss was none other than Deimos Jalencia, who developed the bird mailer system. His expertise in ornithology and access to Marina's expertise in programmable living beings made him a major suspect.

Within hours, every media in the world started relaying the photos of Deimos and Marina as the suspects of the kidnap case and announced a hefty compensation for any information that could trace them.

Merjella was not available to defend her case as she was not aware of anything that happened on the land. She was mourning Mimico's death and spending time with her friends Qwerty and Bingo in Seasorg. She was having her own emergency situation, looking to both defend her city and also take the fight to Zypher.

Watching the television anchors screaming for the head of Deimos and Marina, Sandy broke down. Ryan helped her and assured her that Merjella was a righteous lady and that only she could bring the world out of the hole it was in.

He also made no delay in calling up Rosy Parker. He wanted her to keep mum about Merjella and also explained that she was innocent. Rosy did not look much bothered about the issue, and she only promised him that she would stand by him.

Ryan, being a relieved man, tried to contact Merjella. But a knock on his door demanded his attention beforehand. He was surprised when the policemen stormed in even when he peeped at the door to see who was waiting. The cops went about searching the entire place. They then questioned the whereabouts of Marina Jalencia. Ryan replied that he was not aware, but he was taken into custody. The place was thoroughly examined, and they sealed his home. They seized Marina's bag.

The police saw a resemblance between the army of fishes and the arms made for them and the birds that attacked from the air.

'These fishes might be planned to take control over the water,' suggested the cops among themselves.

Sandy was arrested too. Upon enquiry, Ryan insisted to them that they had to question the mayor in order to find the Boss.

The mayor, who was watching over the enquiry, held Ryan by his throat and asked, 'Where is Marina?'

'I don't know where she is. But she will destroy the Boss. Your boss is going to be very upset with you, Mr Smith.'

Jack Smith left the place angrily.

'You are not going to enjoy anything by destroying the world, Mr Ryan. Nor will you be able to control the whole world. No man managed to do that. Ever since your arrest, we haven't yet received any communication from the Boss. That means your odds are high running for the Boss,' said a cop.

'Officer, the Boss claims to be in control of everything. That's what he demonstrated. If I am his man, he would have ordered you to release me by now. If I'm the Boss, you should have found the chief secretary in my place. You are wasting your time, officer. Arrest the mayor, and you will hear from the Boss soon. Didn't you notice what he asked for? Marina, not the Boss. Deimos and Marina are the threat to the Boss. The mayor got rid of Deimos, and now he wants to wipe out Marina danger,' Ryan explained.

The cop simply nodded and left him in the cell.

19

FINAL FIGHT AT SEASQUARE

As the mourning period came to an end, Merjella started preparing for the war at sea. Despite sending repeated requests to Zypher to release the octopuses detained at the Jello Jail, there came no response from Chiro.

With the presence of Zaquella and Mathello, Merjella organized a high-level meeting in Seasorg to finalize the strategies to deal with Zypher. Zaquella helped them with the detailed map of Zypher, and Mathello assisted them by giving inputs about the workings of the minds of malojels.

As they came up with a decisive final plan, Merjella wanted to keep Ryan informed. But they were unable to reach Ryan, and so they just left a message for him.

Merjella thought it was not prudent to delay things as the loss of Mimico itself was huge and they needed to save the remaining folks. On the new-moon day, Merjella organized the army towards Zypher, ready to battle out, as the Chironers left them with no better choices.

Bingo and Qwerty went along too, along with the army of archerfish, flying fish, and mantis shrimps. As the army comprising millions marched towards Zypher, it brought shudders to the fish world. Zypher was alerted, and they held an emergency meeting to deal with the situation.

'Their army is huge. We cannot fight to win against them,' opined General Datty, a tiger fish.

'But still we can keep them at bay, Chiro,' said the blobfish, who was the chief advisor of Chiro. King Chiro looked at him in a manner suggesting him to continue. 'Stop the army from entering our kingdom. Arrange for a fight with Jella at the Seasquare,' Blob explained.

'Jella is a jellopus, Blob! We can't win a fight against her. She is stronger than a thousand of us together.'

'Yes, she is. But let us tweak a few rules to our advantage. And we will still win. Do not forget the fact that we won this kingdom, getting rid of many jellopuses, Chiro. And Jella is just one jellopus. We will still win.'

Chiro agreed to the plan. The Chironers, comprised of tiger fish and swordfish, stood at the entrance to Zypher. Blob, Caruki, and Aurelia were on Chiro's side at the city gate, awaiting the arrival of the Seasorgans.

The grand army, with all their sophisticated weapons, reached the gates of Zypher and stopped a few feet away. Chiro sent Caruki to convey his invitation to Merjella for a fight at Seasquare.

Merjella discussed with her ministers before agreeing to the fight. As she moved forwards to enter Seasquare, her army followed too. Caruki stopped the army from entering the city and conveyed that the invite was only for Merjella and that only diplomats were allowed to witness the fight. Merjella's army protested the idea, but she pacified them. She then ordered them to stay right there at the gate and instructed them not to enter unless they get their orders.

'But keep alert, soldiers!' said Merjella.

Merjella then proceeded with Bingo, Qwerty, Zaquella, and Mathello to the Seasquare. Aurelia welcomed Merjella to Zypher, and both were delighted to meet for the first time after having heard a lot about each other. They hugged to show their love and support for one another.

The Seasquare was made ready for the fight between Merjella and Nomura. Both of them got on to the square rock and got themselves introduced to the audience. The octopuses were brought to the square too to witness the fight. They erupted in joy on seeing Merjella and started to wave their arms at her. Merjella too waved back.

Caruki was named the referee of the contest, and he started with announcing the rules and regulations. After reading out the regular codes, Blob added, 'The winner will be the one who takes control of the enemy and hold him tight until Caruki taps the rock to the count of three. And it is forbidden to kill anyone in the Kingdom of Zypher. So killing the opponent will call for your disqualification. If Jella wins this bout, then Chiro will declare the release of the inmates of the Jello Jail. And if she loses, she will be arrested, and her army will withdraw from here immediately. Do you both agree?'

Both Merjella and Nomura nodded in acceptance and shook arms with each other.

Chiro took Blob to a corner and discussed with him personally. 'What have you done? I want Jella to be killed, and that's the only way we can be safe, Blob.'

'No, Chiro. You are wrong. If we kill Jella here, then the army waiting outside will come strong on us. Zypher will be destroyed in no time. We have to take custody of Jella and drive them away.'

'But what if the Seasorgans still attack us when we arrest Jella?'

'You don't have to worry about that. Jellopuses live by their words. That is the reason you were able to trounce Tarjo.'

Chiro was convinced by those words, and he allowed the fight to start. As the two contestants were ready to strike each other, Blob declared the start of the fight, and Caruki signalled them to go ahead.

Merjella and Nomura took two diagonal corners and stared at each other. From there, they moved towards each other and collided almost at the centre of the ring. Being a humongous mass of flesh, Nomura managed to push Merjella down to the ground. Before she could blink her eyes, Nomura got hold of her with his several tentacles and started to suffocate her.

Even as Nomura held on with the arm-twisting position, exerting as much pressure as he could for quite a few minutes, Merjella garnered some strength and managed to push him away. She then slowly moved away and took support from the twine rope. She struggled to get her breath back.

With the conical wentletrap shell in his arm, Blob announced, 'The one who falls away from the square rock will be declared defeated.'

Jella looked puzzled at the new rule. Nomura took a long stride away, and in a fast pace, he came rushing and took a long leap to reach Jella, who was leaning on the rope; he thudded on her with an even bigger force. Merjella absorbed the collision and clung on to the ropes with her arms repeatedly crisscrossing the ropes. As Nomura kept on building pressure, the rope gave up, and both lost their balance. While Merjella held on to the rock, Nomura could not find any support, and he slipped out of the rock.

The octopuses shouted in triumph. Jella limped to climb to the top of the rock and raised two of her arms in delight on reaching the centre of the rock. Zaquella and Mathello hugged each other. Qwerty enjoyed the victory in her own style, planting numerous pecks on Bingo.

Blob reached out for his microphone and said, 'Since the rope broke, we cannot declare a winner here. So the fight continues.'

Nomura slowly reached the top of the rock. Merjella wasted no time and pounded Nomura with all her eight arms. Nomura lost his balance and fell on the rock. As Jella held him together and took control of him, instead of quickly counting to three, Caruki circled them as if he was looking for some detail. He then leisurely reached the rock and tapped slowly as Jella held him tightly. By the time he counted two, Nomura pushed Merjella away and came to consciousness.

Jella did not allow Nomura to gain ground as she kept smacking him black and blue. Nomura started to bleed on his head, and he was in pain. Merjella locked Nomura with her arms spun with his and pushed him to the rock's bottom. Caruki did not bother to tap to three even as Jella was expending her energy to hold the strong Nomura. Jella could not believe her eyes. She had heard about malojels and their ways. But that was the first time she was experiencing it herself. She looked broken, realizing that there would be no way she could win the bout.

Soon, Nomura gained strength and bashed Merjella to the ground. As Jella was falling to the ground, she only knew she had to summon all her strength just to keep the fight alive. Nomura pushed himself on her and held on to the rock. Caruki was so fast and started to count, tapping his arm over the rock. He was fast with the count, but Merjella's reflexes came to her help faster. She moved in time, and she tried to push Nomura to the bottom. He resisted and pushed Merjella back down, and the moment she touched the bottom, Caruki started to count. Jella held tight and rolled Nomura to the bottom, and then they started to repeat the sequence faster and faster. Merjella and Nomura were rolling on the rock in a pace that made it hard for the audience to follow who was at the bottom and who had the upper hand.

Then at one point, Merjella gave up and Nomura held her firmly, staying on top of her. Caruki did not think twice to count. As he counted to three, the hearts of octopuses missed a beat. There was complete silence.

Caruki lifted one of the arms of Nomura to announce him as the winner. While raising the arms, Nomura turned to Merjella.

'And please, give a big hand to the winner today!' Caruki raised his arms and shockingly saw that he was holding Merjella's arm.

The whole crowd gave a thundering applause to the winner. And when Caruki looked down at the rock, it was Nomura who was struggling to regain his breath. The furious Chiro rushed to the square rock. Aurelia followed too with the same urgency.

While gasping heavily, Nomura told Chiro, 'Caruki disobeyed your orders . . .'

Chiro seemed like he did not want to hear more from Nomura. His sucker punch got rid of the struggling Nomura with ease. Chiro then moved fast towards Merjella. Aurelia intervened and stopped him from advancing.

Chiro ordered his troops to arrest Aurelia for treason. But nobody moved. He glared at Blob.

Blob said, 'We can't kill Jella and then escape the wrath of the huge army waiting at our doors. Such action will ruin the prospects of Zypher. Moreover, your authority as the king of Zypher is over the moment your Nomura lost to Jella. Now we can't take orders from you, Chiro.'

'What, Blob? Since when was he my Nomura? He was always our Nomura, wasn't he?'

'It was never like that, Chiro. It was always you and yours here in Zypher ever since you got rid of the great Tarjo,' Aurelia told Chiro. She then turned to the Chironers and commanded, 'Arrest him,' pointing at Chiro.

The Chironers looked at one another while General Datty came forward to arrest Chiro.

Merjella crowned Aurelia as the queen of Zypher in front of the gathering. She then ordered the release of all the prisoners and announced a special celebration for the return of the jellopus. Merjella honoured the occasion by attending the ceremony.

20

EYECANDY ATTACKED

Mail after mail from the Boss was delivered to the International Council. Each one carried instructions that had to be followed.

The Boss declared the whole world to be his property and wanted to tax each country according to the area they occupied. He also directed the nations to establish an embassy for him. He wanted the nations to declare their assets of natural resources and pay 5 per cent of the resources to him immediately. He targeted oil and precious metals.

The Boss also ordered the nations not to build any military units as he not only found that a threat to his supremacy but also feared that any war would cause damage to the natural resources and that would in turn affect his profitability. He set a date for the world nations to ensure closure of all battalions. He also demanded the shutting down of research and development of any form.

'What is he? What does he want? It is hard to understand' was the comment from a staff.

'Ask him about the chief secretary. Ask him to release Mr Moses immediately,' General Martin said.

The International Council did establish an emergency squad with talented officers and soldiers. They named the team as Bird Team. A team of specialists from various departments represented the panel, which was headed by General Alex Martin.

'Ask him to identify himself,' he added.

'There is no doubt, General. It is Deimos Jalencia. His past records are not clean as well. Though there is no direct evidence pointing at him, he still is a suspect on many cases. His turbulent childhood adds to the suspicion,' explained Mike Jones, a psychologist who served Kreppo Police Department. 'He was involved in drug trafficking and was last seen in Blueshells along with his wife Marina Jalencia. She is a scientist as well.'

'What have we got, Dr Jones?' asked the general.

'The Blueshells police have another inventor in custody. He is Ryan Catchmore. He is famous for his fishing gears. The police also seized a lot of fishes and weapons that have been designed to be used underwater. There is enough evidence to prove that they have plans to gain control in the water as well. Like birds in the air, they might be planning to use those fishes underwater.'

'Do we have any other name to be suspected to have a hand in this? What if we are facing a new enemy? What if he is not Deimos? What if it's someone more powerful?' said General Martin.

'But Deimos is very powerful, no doubt,' replied the psychologist.

'I don't see any motive here, Dr Jones!'

'As a child, he was abused by many. Having lost his mother early, he was subjected to a rough life by his stepmother and uncles and even his half brother, who is younger to him. He was physically abused all throughout his childhood. He was very helpless, and when he enjoys the power, he wants to apply it to the extreme,' explained Dr Jones.

'Mmmm . . .' There was a pause in the hall. 'Forget about attacking him. We haven't yet located him. What are our defensive options, Lieutenant?'

'The only option we have is to shoot down all the birds.'

The crew passed that option like a dosage of laughter.

'Come on, men! This is no joke,' said Lieutenant Harper.

'That is not fair, Lieutenant!' condemned the environmentalist in the panel.

'We are in danger. Human life is the top priority.'

'Hunting down the birds may be a temporary solution, Lieutenant. Tomorrow it will be in the form of animals or humans. Are we prepared to kill everyone? Who is going to live then?' questioned the general himself. He had everyone do the thinking.

It was then that a soldier entered in with some documents. 'General! We got a satellite picture locating the supposed place of the Boss. It is on an island. It is near where the base station lost the signal from the two choppers that followed the birds. There are also heavy activities of birds detected there,' the soldier presented the report to General Martin.

There was a sigh of relief following the discovery. But the job was not yet over.

They called for more-detailed satellite pictures of the place. The island was Eyecandy. It was a private island owned by a sixty-year-old billionaire, Russell Bond. His business included oil refineries and mining. He sold off his business and retired a decade ago. He had not been seen ever since. He was enjoying his retired life in Eyecandy, which was developed into a completely independent state. It generated its own electricity and had all the infrastructures. The island had good access to essential things.

The first order from the Bird Team was to stop all civil supplies to Eyecandy. Then they charted out ways to attack the island and take control. As a first step, they sent a cruiser to inform Russell Bond about the plan to attack the island if he failed to surrender in the next twelve hours. But the cruiser was denied entry to Eyecandy, and they were warned and sent back. The shore was completely electric-fenced, making it impossible to enter without destroying them.

The Bird Team chalked out the plan to storm the island. They overlooked the security of Calvin Moses as they thought the danger was much more than the safety of one man. They planned to surround the island with six ships and take twenty helicopters of soldiers for the terrestrial attack. Another ten jet fighters were placed, ready for bombing if necessary.

The troops got ready. The army men were very enthusiastic and proud about going for a worthy fight. They never seemed to need any motivation. They were all naturally charged up.

The choppers slowly neared Eyecandy. From the aerial view, the island resembled a wide-open eye. It was such a beautiful island surrounded by clear bluish-green water. It had well-laid roads and was filled with palm trees. The helicopters went in a line. The first one took position and was about to land. The moment it went closer by about a few metres from ground, it was powerfully thrown away. The out-of-control chopper hit the nose of the second one tailing her. Both helicopters spun a dozen times before crashing and hitting the water.

That warned the soldiers and the commanders in charge. They called off the helicopters and returned back to the base. The orders were sent to the ships and jet fighters to bomb the island ruthlessly. But they were stunned at what they were witnessing. The bombs bounced off and scattered into all other directions and were blasted away. Two of their own ships were completely destroyed in that attack. They had to retreat.

The Bird Team had their options drained out. They soon felt being in a situation where they were mere spectators of what was about to happen. Their only option left was to wait for the next mail from the Boss. They waited for his instructions as if they conceded to him as their boss.

Even before any communication from the supposedly agitated Boss, the Bird Team was subjected to severe blasting from their own leaders for attacking Eyecandy without measuring the levels of danger.

The Boss was not late either.

Dear General Martin,

I'm impressed. You spotted me and attacked in quick time. But now the Boss is very upset.

Shut down immediately the military bases and any kind of research operations in all the countries. I have not attacked anyone till now. But I have to do this.

Kindly see the file attached.

Furiously yours,
The Boss

The mail came with a video file attachment. The visual was of the chief secretary of the International Council, Calvin Moses, who was kneeling and pleading for mercy as one of the goons held his neck at knife point. He was already bleeding in his mouth and forehead. It was a sickening sight.

They soon ordered the shutting down of all military operations. The Bird Team was relocated to a secret locality and was only employed to make progress in the investigation but not to authorize any more attacks. They were barred even from arresting anyone with regards to the issue.

After organizing Seasorg and Zypher, Merjella went back to Blueshells, needing to settle her scores on land. She was puzzled to see Ryan's house sealed and surrounded by tight security. She could think of none other than Rosy Parker for information.

She should know everything, Merjella said to herself.

Rosy was all smiles at seeing Merjella home. She welcomed her and made her feel at home. She went inside and brought her things to contain her hunger.

Rosy claimed innocence about the whereabouts of Ryan. Merjella was not convinced with such an answer from Rosy. She then asked her about Sandy's house, and Rosy offered to take her there. Mrs Parker made Merjella wait for some time so that she would get ready. The police promptly arrived in quick time to arrest Merjella. Rosy gestured to Merjella that she had no choice.

At the police headquarters, Merjella learnt everything—from the kidnapping of the chief secretary of the International Council to the vain attack on Eyecandy. Before any enquiry was made, the Blueshells Police Department received instructions to release Ryan and all others who were arrested in connection to the case of the Boss. The order was a result of the state's efforts to pacify the Boss.

As they came out of the prison, there were about four speeding cars that stopped in front of them with screeching noises. Before they realized what was happening, there were random gunshots at them. Merjella disappeared at once, but Ryan and Sandy succumbed to the bullets and fell dead.

Merjella pushed the time back till they were about to walk out of the prison. She made herself invisible, along with Ryan and Sandy too. The prison doors were opened, and the speeding cars came to a screeching halt. But no bullets were fired. The gunmen in the car waited with their guns pointed at the doors.

Merjella moved near the cars. The mayor was sighted in one of the cars. As the invisible Merjella opened his car door, the gang was shocked at seeing the door open automatically. In a whisk, Merjella slit open the throat of Jack Smith.

The invisible Ryan said to the dying mayor, 'I did warn you.'

21

DAYS OF LOVE

Returning to Ryan's home, Merjella easily broke open the sealed doors. The place was completely ransacked with the fish tanks broken into pieces. There were no traces of fishes left. The garage was totally destroyed too. The whole place needed a complete facelift. For Merjella, it was easily done than said. With a wave of her hand, she brought order to the house.

Even as time was running out, they sat down to discuss. They had very little information, and unfortunately, they had no idea about where to get the information they needed. They had an argument over the killing of the mayor. Ryan thought they should have caught hold of him and pressed for information.

'I don't think he would have revealed anything. If he is important, the Boss would go more offensive, and if he is not, then Smith might not know much,' said Merjella.

'Sometimes you are very aggressive, Merjella,' said Ryan.

There was a momentary silence. Sandy brought them lemonades.

'To me, this battle we have on land is more important, and you should forget about your revenge plans at sea. You should give me enough time to come up with an idea,' remarked Ryan.

'The sea battle was long over, Ryan. We have defeated the malojels and crowned Aurelia as the queen of Zypher. We tried contacting you, but you were not available.'

'Wow. That's very good news, Merjella,' said Sandy excitedly.

'Oh, that's amazing!' Ryan blushed and added, 'You should've informed us of that earlier. I would've focused my energy long back on this terror on land.'

'Well, you can start focusing now.'

They heard a knock at the door. Sandy volunteered to answer the door, but Merjella stopped her.

'Do not answer the door. I shall do that,' said Merjella and proceeded to the door. She turned herself invisible before she opened the door. They were the Bird Team members. They were a little surprised to see no one at the opened door. But Merjella appeared right before them. General Martin showed his identity card, and they gained entrance into the house.

They were greeted with warm hospitality. Since they were all running out of time, they went straight to the issue.

'My intuition tells me you are not the Boss's men,' started the general. 'We initially believed Deimos is the Boss. But then, it turned out to be Russell Bond, a billionaire in his own right. Still we believe Deimos is in the background. And none other than Marina can help us better unknot this situation,' said Lieutenant Harper.

'Deimos has long been killed by the Boss's men,' started Merjella, and she went on with her story that she remembered thus far.

The team looked a little disappointed about not achieving any kind of breakthrough. They showed her the satellite pictures of Eyecandy and videos of the attack on the island. She felt that the place was very familiar and asked for more visuals.

The aerial view of Eyecandy shown to her helped her remember her first look at the island a few years back.

'Deimos! Wow, what a beautiful place!' That was exactly how Marina saw the island first from a private jet at a few metres of altitude while they were preparing to land on the island.

That was the place Deimos wanted to take Marina to for their first outing. He knew Eyecandy could amaze any girl in this world. It was a private island of just more than a few hundred square miles. Surprisingly, it had good roads, a posh house in the centre, a huge helipad, and also a runway for private jets to land. It had the complete infrastructure that a country needs and with plenty of staff. Deimos earned access to Eyecandy through Russell Bond, who owned that island.

Apart from the scenic beauty of that place, it became a very memorable spot for Marina because of the first kiss she had there. She pitied herself for having to labour too much to remember such a memorable event.

Though they started dating much earlier, this was the place Deimos reserved for the occasion. Their first date happened a few months earlier. They went around Pynto, the busiest city in the entire world. Deimos took her to the famous Garden of Glory, which housed all kinds of rare as well as ornamental plants. Deimos knew very well about the things that would interest Marina. That helped him carefully plan the date. They visited the theatre and witnessed a delightful stage act. They then had a long walk through the central park of the city before calling it a day. It would have been a complete day for Marina had

Deimos kissed her. It did not happen that day. Maybe Deimos had different plans.

They did meet a few more times before their trip to Eyecandy. Deimos had always been nice to her, and that was unexpected as they were rivals at work.

They had first met at the annual science convention held at Pynto. It was a prestigious event happening every year to felicitate the scientists from all over the world for their contributions. It was indeed prestigious for scientists to win prizes at that event. Deimos and Marina were both strong contenders that year. They did not converse with each other much, but they both assumed the other one would not entertain their presence there.

Deimos was there with his innovative bird mailer service. He used birds to send and receive letters. A bird was first placed on an induced environment in a box for about five minutes. A code would be generated for the induced environment. The bird would then be taken out, and the letter or package to be delivered would be tied to it. The recipient would be provided with the code, and he should apply that code to create the environment in the box provided to him. The bird would then fly the shortest route to the destination and deliver the letter or package.

Though it was applauded a lot by a section of the scientists, some argued that that was just an extension of an old concept. They cited that the pigeons were used in olden days in a similar fashion. But they all agreed to the fact that the simulation of the environment was new, and it would help ease transportation. They thought that technique would help in military assignments very much.

Marina's project was with plants. She was successful in injecting microchips in plants and then controlling various biological activities in them. She was able to program their activities that included plant growth, the flowering process and pollination, and even the quantity of yield on a particular day. It amazed the science enthusiasts, and they called that a revolutionary technology.

Marina demonstrated that on mango plants in various stages. She had installed the chips in those plants and connected that with a touchscreen monitor. The monitor, which was connected to its stem, indicated the exact number of mangoes in the tree and also provided the estimates. The estimates included the number of fruits that would ripen on a particular day on a normal course. She then successfully demonstrated delaying the ripening of fruits so that they can be had as one would wish. She also demonstrated controlling the growth of the plant as a whole and also controlling other critical processes of the plant too.

Everyone felt that was a good concept to avoid wastages and also a way to extend the season of certain vegetables and fruits. That also gave some hope in growing any plant in any condition.

Despite other valuable contributions from other great scientists, those two from Deimos and Marina were considered groundbreaking ones that year. Their odds too were almost evenly placed in the betting world, with a slight edge for Marina.

The evening before the results were expected to be announced, Deimos met Marina.

She had lost both her parents in a mine accident in Histan only recently, and Marina stayed back at her room even as the other young scientists were touring the beautiful city of Pynto. She was in her casual night pants and printed shirt when Deimos knocked at her door. He was wearing a formal suit in black.

That was their first meeting—their first meeting in private. When Marina answered the door, from outside her room, Deimos presented her with a bouquet of beautiful red flowers.

'Your work is very impressive. I am afraid I will only be second to you,' admitted Deimos.

'Whoever wins tomorrow, I doubt neither of our work would be second to none,' replied the modest Marina, who did not want to concede too.

Deimos was impressed by her choice of words. He stood at the door, expecting Marina to invite him inside, but that did not happen. The casualness of Marina wooed Deimos, and at the same time, Deimos's gentleman approach attracted her. He then invited her for dinner that night, and she obliged.

Marina carefully chose her outfit for dinner. She picked a red-and-white skirt and a sleeveless top. She painted her lips rose and wore heart-shaped red earrings. Her neck was covered with a glittering platinum necklace with red stones embedded in it.

Deimos was waiting for her at the table, and he was in the same dress in which he had met her an hour earlier. It was as though he arrived straight at the restaurant after inviting her.

They spent quite a valuable time that night, discussing at length about all kinds of topics ranging from world politics to local sports.

They both showed mutual respect and shared more ideas about developing the other's work. They both wanted to work together, but neither expressed it. They both felt that it was too early to spill out their desires.

That meeting changed both their lives. It made them both meet again and again and again. They soon started to date, and it was then that Deimos made a plan to take her to Eyecandy. Marina was not aware of where Deimos was planning to take her. All she knew was that she accepted the request from Deimos to accompany him for a few days. And then they were at the island called Eyecandy.

Marina knew nothing about the island prior to that visit. They both had much fun there. They stayed in the palace that was located in the centre of the island. Deimos enjoyed a royal reception during their brief stay. He only mentioned to her that the island was his boss's. She was in the dark about his boss.

Eyecandy was closed to the public and other tourists. There was a private security force in place to protect the island from intruders. The island did have abundant oil and energy resources. Deimos did take Marina to the refineries and explained to her about the potential of the island to survive independently. Apart from that, the island did have a few windmills and electricity grids that helped supply uninterrupted power to the whole of the island round the clock.

The whole island looked completely explored and well planned for a beautiful undisturbed life. The beaches were long and clean. There was a feel of romance and freshness always in the air.

'I would have named it Heaven on Earth,' said Merjella to the Bird Team.

'But today you will have to rethink that,' differed General Martin. They then briefed her about the latest developments. 'If we have the technology behind your pro-dog, we may be able to find a solution to stop these atrocities,' said the general.

'I'm afraid I may not be able to help you with that. I can rework on that, but it would take a long time. All the papers were stolen at Mayor Smith's place. You can make a search there if that will help.'

'I am afraid we don't have time for that now. We have to stop the Boss. We have to capture Eyecandy and put an end to this new terror,' said the lieutenant sternly.

'I can find a way to enter Eyecandy. But brief me about the military actions taken on Eyecandy,' volunteered Merjella.

Lieutenant Harper provided her with all the information.

'It seems they have created a shield on their island that produces a strong repulsive force if it comes into contact with an intruder, making it almost impossible to enter,' inferred Merjella, listening to them.

'Yes. You are right. We thought they generated their own gravitational force for their island, and we felt there should be some kind of escape velocity to penetrate the layer. So we tried launching supersonic missiles, hypersonic jets, and even objects at high hypersonic speeds into the island, but no success.'

'They have created a layer that defies earth's gravity,' suggested Ryan.

'That cannot be. If they negated the gravity of earth, then all the objects in Eyecandy should be floating,' said Merjella.

'The threat is intensifying at a rapid pace. The Boss had already engaged programmed monkeys into the research stations and military facilities of the surrendered nations. He has taken complete control,' explained Harper.

As they were brainstorming, Bingo called up. The flip-model phone made to look like a beautiful oyster shell rang as well as lighting red. A red call denoted an emergency call, and Merjella picked it up. Bingo informed Merjella that there were cold-blooded attacks on humans going into the sea.

'We have located a place near a shore in the south-west direction to Zypher from where viperfish are being released. The place is well protected and have multiple gates,' informed Bingo.

'That should be the shores of Eyecandy. We will have to rush.' Merjella left for the sea in a hurry, accompanied by Ryan and Sandy.

22

BREAKING INTO EYECANDY

By the time they reached the sea, the news had spread that all kinds of vessels in the sea were being attacked and destroyed by aggressive viperfish. They could see from the shore that fishing boats of various sizes were crumbling into the sea. Merjella took her time to assess the situation.

They decided against taking their boat to enter the sea. As Merjella helped Ryan and Sandy get fins, they simply walked into the sea and started to swim. On their way to Seasorg, they witnessed the attack going on in the sea. They saw viperfish attacking like they were possessed by some evil spirit.

They attacked the boats in groups, and after they succeeded in capsizing the boats, they spread out and attacked the sailors venomously. They bit and tore them apart. And once the blood oozed out, sharks did the rest of the ritual.

The beautiful seabed was fast getting deglamourized by the accumulation of the remains of boats and ships and the clothes and accessories of fishermen.

Ryan, who was not willing to be led, swam ahead on his own. On his way, he bumped into a group of viperfish. For a second, his heart thought that it is of no use to function any more and stopped pumping. He stood frozen in that chilly seawater. As Sandy and Merjella watched, the viperfish did not bother to make a mince out of him. Still his heart waited for the whole large group to pass him before getting restarted for its job.

'The fins saved him,' remarked Sandy.

'They should be programmed to attack only the humans. Fishes are spared,' Merjella explained.

Though Merjella wanted to get rid of those thousands of fish on an attacking spree in the sea, she had to proceed with the much needed task of the hour. She needed to locate the source of the evil and put an end to the global seizure as early as possible.

They soon reached Seasorg and were taken immediately to their military facility. They were shown live feeds of the Seasorg Army stationed at the borders of Eyecandy.

They were watching the release of viperfish through the three-layer security chamber. There were three doors, and each company of viperfish passed through them together. Only one door remained open at a time.

When the first door was opened, the fish moved to the first duct all together. Then the door closed, and the chambers were scrutinized. The empty second chamber was lit in red while inspection went on and turned to green as soon as it was found intruder-free. Then they were all sent into that second chamber by opening the middle gate. Again inspection went on before the gravity screen for that opening was temporarily withheld. The final exit was then opened, and the viperfish were released into the sea.

While a batch of viperfish were coming out, a Seasorgan zebra fish managed to go past the gate and reach the second duct. Immediately after the company of viperfish exited into the sea, the gate was closed, and the gravity shield was turned on. And the scanning began. The zebra fish was detected and was shot down with no investigation into the matter. The exit duct was then readied for the next batch of viperfish to make their exit into the sea.

'The borders are completely locked from trespassers. We may not be able to enter without breaking their shield,' declared Macko-Whack, the captain of a mantis shrimp squad.

Merjella wanted to learn about how the gravity shield was created. There was not any clue to find out what were used to create the effect of gravity. The Seasorgans continued to research the whole area. Whenever any of them reached close to the border, they would be pushed away by a great repulsive force and sometimes it resulted in fatal damages.

With viperfish attacking recklessly at sea, several teams of ribbonfish and mantis shrimps were carrying out the investigative operation deep in the sea. The ribbonfish carefully scanned through the place as the mantis shrimps were made to touch the 'devil's cloud' and get thrown away. They tried to locate the place where the disturbance was high when the shield reacted. After a long search, they found something that could be a potential clue to their questions.

'We see a short metallic pipe-like structure erected at the bottom of the seabed with the help of concrete,' Macko-Whack conveyed to the control room in Seasorg's military headquarters.

The team at the control room sensed that as a breakthrough in sight.

'Shall we take a look at those structures?' Merjella requested.

A mantis shrimp soldier took out the camera and fixed that on to one of his eyes. Merjella started to get the video feed of the place on the giant screen she was watching.

Macko-Whack went near the metal piece and swung his raptorial claws at the piece at a rapid pace. He was thrown back with a much bigger momentum. Macho-Whack fell down a few feet away after swirling in the water upon impact. His subordinates rushed to help him.

'Macko . . . Macko . . . are you okay?' asked Merjella from the control room.

The grounded Macko-Whack slowly moved and adjusted his microphone and answered, 'Yes, I am all right. We are up against a tough proposition.'

'Do not try to destroy anything unless we give you definite orders. How many such structures have you spotted so far?'

'This thing was embedded skilfully and is concealed in the seabed. Not easy to spot. So far we have spotted only one.'

'There should be more around the island if that's the device we are looking for. If we can't find more than this one, then this may not be the object. Keep searching.'

After employing several ribbonfish patrols in that area, they discovered that there were many such structures placed at uniform distances of about a few metres running around the whole island.

Ryan explained, 'Those structures may emit high-energy ions and run through all kinds of mediums, be it water or air. There should be a very high tower at the centre of the island that is equipped with reflectors—maybe a huge spherical reflector that will reflect these ions back to the source in all directions. These ions should travel at an enormous velocity that whatever comes into contact are thrown back at a faster speed.'

'You are a genius, Ryan. Do we need to destroy the big tower to get rid of this devil's cloud?' asked Merjella.

'Yes, Merjella! You are right. There may not be other options. But we can do that only if we enter the island.'

'Can we try destroying these embedded pipes in the seabed?' Bingo suggested.

'But how are we going to do that? We can't use force to destroy it. Without force, how can we destruct a thing?' Ryan questioned back.

'Implosives,' said Sandy.

'What?' exclaimed Ryan.

'We should try implosives. Implode the concrete that holds those metal pipes. That should open them up.'

'Excellent idea, Sandy,' praised Merjella.

Merjella informed Macko-Whack to stay put and that they were on their way. They then rushed to the border with an implosives team. The sight of the deep sea was still the same, with only increased incidents of the attacks going on. Once the team reached the spot, they inspected the place. Merjella ordered the army to switch to the offensive stance and get rid of the viperfish.

Immediately after the orders flew in, the Seasorg Army went on a rampage. They teamed up perfectly to make a successful counterattack. Five flying fish each took a firm grip on viperfish. While the viperfish were still in a panic-ridden state, they were pulled out of the water and flown through the air for a brief phase. As they were about to plunge back into the water, the viperfish were further confused by the strong shots of water jets on their faces, which were from the archerfish. Before they could recover from the assault, they were placed at the seabed, where the mantis shrimps did the final ritual, giving the lethal blow with their raptorial claws in an unfolded position. The moment the punch was delivered, it was all over for the viperfish. The army fast got rid of the viperfish.

Meanwhile, the implosives team, with the assistance of Sandy, planted the implosives in the concrete base of the pipes and imploded the first pipe. The structure collapsed, and this brought cheers to the camp. But to their disappointment, there still existed the cloud, throwing them back.

'Nothing to worry about, Merjella. The effect produced by the adjacent sources should be strong enough to back up the tampered location. We may succeed if we destroy four or five such successive structures,' advised Sandy.

She was proved right, and the shield was broken open by destroying two more structures on either side of the initially broken up pipe. They gained entry into Eyecandy.

23

MERJELLA VERSUS THE BOSS

As soon as the devil's cloud was broken, Merjella, Ryan, and Sandy stormed into the island Eyecandy. From behind the dense bush in that beach area, they watched the movement in the island from a distance. Merjella's memories was beginning to fall into place. She could remember every detail of her previous visit to that island and about her past too. She could hardly figure out any striking difference in the island from her last visit there five or six years ago. The security had not even gotten tighter than how it was on her maiden visit. Upon looking at the place, they knew it was going to be a swift ride for them from then on, with no armed guards around to report their arrival.

Merjella picked up her oyster shell phone to inform the Bird Team about the breach on the barriers of Eyecandy.

'Greetings, General Martin! We have broken into Eyecandy. The south-west frontier of Eyecandy was stripped open a few minutes back. Choppers and jets can now sail through.'

'Congratulations, Marina! We are on the way.'

The three of them looked relieved at the news.

'Guess the Boss overlooked the idea that his gravity shield could be overcome. He should be surprised to find himself without a guard. Here we come, Mr Russell

Bond.' Ryan Catchmore set himself off jauntily towards the palace.

As his feet stamped deeper and deeper into the loose soil of Eyecandy, his advancement was brought to halt by a little sparrow that flew near his face, catching him by surprise. When he looked at the bird, she blew his head off, spitting a tiny bomb on to him. Marina, who was watching from a few yards away, wasted no time in pulling back time and bringing him to where they were just after they made contact with the Bird Team.

'Guess the Boss overlooked the idea that his gravity shield could be overcome. He should be surprised to find himself without a guard. Here we come, Mr Russell Bond.' Ryan Catchmore started to move forward, only to be stopped by Merjella.

'Wait! Don't walk blindly! Stay with us,' instructed Merjella.

'What's wrong with you? Why don't we just walk through this place and save millions of lives?' Ryan protested and tried to make a quick move again.

Merjella got ahead of him and dragged him back before she gave him a tight slap and said, 'If you are not going to show patience, neither will I!'

Merjella turned everyone invisible—visible only amongst themselves—and led them to the palace. Meanwhile, there was quite a bustle in the secret facility from where the Bird Team was operating.

The jittery face of General Martin suggested that things were not encouraging despite the call from Merjella. Apart from that one positive news, there were hundreds of unfavourable developments from around the world that kept pouring into the station.

The eagles and viperfish were bringing down all man-made objects that were flying and floating. They had almost lost all aircrafts and were forced to ground the remaining few ones. So was the case with naval vessels as well. The world nations were all surrendering to the Boss one after another, and soon it would be a question of whom the Bird Team would be fighting for.

Despite the knowledge that Eyecandy had been breached, General Martin was unable to commission a fighter plane to attack since no airborne vehicle was safe. The eagles were in complete control of the air space. And some eagles started to attack the civilians of yet-to-surrender nations and looted the belongings irrespective of what they were. The lootings included anything from fruits and vegetables to precious ornaments.

With all those acquisitions, eagles were busy reporting to the air base of Eyecandy. Merjella and her mates watched the eagles coming in large numbers and handing over their plunders to the officials. The valuables were then sorted and moved to their respective repositories.

Remaining in stealth mode, Merjella, Ryan and Sandy passed through the air base to reach the palace. The palace housed a big tower with a shining metal ball at the top, which should be the 'devil's sphere'. The palace was well protected but with limited human force. There were three lions doing rounds. They were ready to feast on anything that was not wearing the uniform and the badge.

The staff were dressed in a baggy green uniform with a dull yellow collar. The badge was circular and contained a simple logo—equilateral triangles pointing upwards. Though that looked simple, it was made of platinum plate with class A diamonds embedded in it, making that too expensive to duplicate. The badge also contained the line 'The Boss'.

They reached the palace doors that were kept wide open. The huge front hall of the palace was decorated with beautiful young girls dressed in attires from various worlds. That should please any man belonging to any generation, any region, and any belief.

Merjella felt it was time for them to get into action.

'Sandy, Ryan, you both go this way and find Mr Mosses and other prisoners if any,' Merjella commanded them, pointing her finger at the long corridor that led to a large number of rooms. She wanted to reach the control room and release the programmed control over the animals.

Sandy signalled Merjella to be silent as she thought that would let the guards know that there were intruders around.

'No! No! Never worry. Like they can't see us, they won't be able to hear us too.'

'Why didn't you tell us that before?' Ryan posed.

'Because, when in stress, you won't just keep your mouth shut.'

Ryan started to scream aloud, and he looked like he wanted to vent his stress. Suddenly, he moved towards a guard and slapped him hard, laughing aloud. As the guard got alerted and called for help, Ryan turned around and ran towards Merjella. They all then went inside one of the rooms.

'You gone mad? Why did you hit him?' asked Merjella.

'I thought that like they can't see us and like they can't hear us, they can't feel us too.' Ryan came up with his rationale.

'Oh really! You thought they can't feel you too? Great. I will make it so. From now on, you won't be felt too. You can go around and hit them, smack them. Do all you want.'

'Yes! Yes!' Ryan punched the air in delight.

'Okay, let's move! We have little time!' Merjella rushed out of the room.

Sandy, who was standing close to the door, got out of the room first, and when Merjella got through the door, she pulled the handle and left the door open very little. Ryan, who was following her, got stuck at the door, and when he tried to open the door, he could not. He just could not catch a grip on the door, and he struggled to squeeze past that slender opening.

While Sandy was following Merjella in that long hallway, she turned back to see if Ryan was not far behind. She was a little worried on not seeing him anywhere near.

'What is Ryan doing? Why isn't he following us?' Sandy questioned Merjella.

Merjella stopped walking and looked at Sandy. She then realized what would have happened and rushed back to open the door for Ryan. Ryan was fuming, and he wanted to get back the sense of feeling, but Merjella seemed to not care about his demands.

'Now I shall leave you both on your own. Check all the rooms and find the prisoners. Go ahead.'

When Ryan and Sandy moved, Merjella called to them to say, 'Do not take anyone outside the palace before we take control of the animals. The moment you step outside the palace, the lions will prey on you.'

'Won't they come inside the palace and attack us?' questioned Ryan.

'No, they won't. They should have been programmed not to enter the palace. Anyhow, you will be safe as you are invisible, but the ones who are much more valuable are without that luxury.'

'What did you just say?'

'I said we have come for someone more valuable than you, Mr Catchmore.'

'Oh yeah! That clown who couldn't keep himself safe and lands on this evil island is valuable, and the one who manages to enter this place against all odds holds a lesser tag. Great! And may I know why I am less valued than him despite me being more intellectual, more innovative, and alert enough not to get caught?'

'Well! You were dead already, Ryan! And I brought you back to life! They didn't want to catch you alive, they just killed you. But him, they kept him alive—hopefully. That suggests he has some value. Now, will you still mind moving from here, Mr Catchmore? You are wasting time like it is valueless like you!'

'What! You arrogant fishy maid made of jelly, I can't believe you said all this!'

Sandy tried to pull him away as he was still listing all the words he thought suited Merjella, but she could not get a grip on him. But Merjella had already moved on, and so Ryan was pacified in a few seconds.

Sandy and Ryan moved on to the first room in the pathway while Merjella rushed to the living room, where they were put up in their previous visit.

The room had been converted into a control room. There were six huge television monitors arranged on the wall, constantly running live feeds from all the cameras in the building. As she moved inside the room, passing by the cosy couch, she saw a server room partitioned with glass walls, and to the left were two doors, one leading to the bedroom and the other to the laboratory. She noticed no one was in the room yet.

Merjella entered the server room. She did not find it hard to break into the main server and gain access as there were not much tweaks made to the program she developed along with Deimos for their pro-dogs. She went on to reach the command page where they could plant orders on the animals. She could see a list of animals and the orders they had been imposed with. She withdrew those orders one by one.

As she withdrew the attack mode on the eagles, they stopped attacking people and resumed their usual behaviour. And when she withdrew the order on the viperfish, they stopped attacking the sailors and fishermen at sea. And when she restored the lions to normal, they wasted no time attacking a couple of guards in uniform and tearing them into pieces. They then ran into the wild, dragging their food.

The Bird Team that was closely monitoring the developments was convinced that things had come back to normal and that the time was up for them to attack. General Martin ordered a fleet to Eyecandy.

While Merjella withdrew the offensive stances, the alarm went up, signalling on the huge monitor that the security level was down below the critical level. She started to pluck out the wires to shut down the entire room. When she pulled the lever on the backup power and as the systems all died out, she felt that there was something behind her and she turned back to look.

Merjella turned back to see Deimos rushing out of the bedroom door, fuming, 'What the hell is going on?' He hurried towards the server room.

Deimos! the shocked Merjella said to herself. She rushed towards Deimos, and as both reached the door, Merjella gave a hard slap to his face. He fell down, crying for help.

'Who are you? Who . . . who . . . who are you?' Deimos stuttered, trying to stand up.

He ran into the laboratory. In a hurry, he searched the tools drawer and reached out for the thermal goggles. He pulled out the gun from his waist sleeve and came out of the room, shouting, 'Come to me now! Come! Come!'

With the thermal goggles on, Deimos could see Merjella's position, but he could not identify her. He could see only the thermal map of her through the goggles, and he started shooting at her aggressively. Merjella, in a whisk, changed to a housefly and flew. Deimos was unable to track her down, so he pulled the trigger randomly.

After some time, when he was done with the bullets in his hand, Merjella became visible to him and punched him heavily on his face. He collapsed to the ground, and she pulled his goggles away to allow him to see her.

Deimos was on the floor, limping to reach the bedroom door. He was shocked to see Merjella.

'Marina . . .'

'Yes, Marina!'

He grinned shamelessly at her. Disgusted to see his smile, Merjella stamped her foot on his chin. Recovering from the strike, Deimos held his chin by his right hand and asked her to stop by hiding his face with his left hand.

'Stop it, Marina. Stop it. We will make a deal.'

Merjella kicked him again, but he managed to block with his left hand. Merjella still kicked him with her other foot on his face, which he failed to see coming.

Deimos started to bleed on his nose, and he was lying helpless. Merjella moved a step closer to him, and the bedroom door opened again. A three-year-old boy came out of the door with a cute puppy doll in his hand and a thin blue satin cloth wrapped around him. The boy seemed to have come straight from sleep.

Seeing Deimos down, the boy ran to him and held him.

'Dad!' the boy called to Deimos.

'Louis, Louis . . .' Deimos pulled him close into his chest.

'Who is this child, Deimos?' asked Merjella, who looked terribly shocked.

Deimos grinned. 'Louis is our child, Marina.'

Merjella stood devastated.

He turned to the boy and said, 'Louis! This is your mother, Marina.' He smiled again.

'Are there any wrong deeds you haven't done so far, Deimos? How could you lie to me about his existence?'

'I never lied, Marina. I told you clearly then.' While on the conversation, Deimos was slowly reaching to the knife he had hidden in his belt.

'Told what?'

'That you were not lucky. And neither are you now!' Giving an evil smile, Deimos pulled the knife and was about to stab Louis's neck.

Merjella was not far away to catch his hand. She arm-twisted his right hand that was holding the knife and stabbed his neck from the backside with his own hand. The boy kept hitting Merjella's legs to make her let go of his dad.

As Deimos fell to the ground dead, Merjella lifted Louis up. She kissed his cheeks and held him tightly into her shoulders. When she turned to see the door, the soldiers sent by the Bird Team marched in.

'Madam, are you okay?' asked one of them.

Merjella nodded her head and walked out. Ryan and Sandy were waiting for her by the palace doors. They seemed to have already handed over Calvin Moses to the army. Moses thanked Merjella for her brave actions.

An old man holding a walking stick walked to Merjella. There were obvious marks on his face and skin from being tortured.

'You are a lovely girl,' said the old man.

'And you are?' asked Merjella. The little boy was standing with Merjella.

'I'm Russell Bond. I was once greedy. My greed was to live a luxurious life alone. I chose this beautiful island. I picked my staff with utmost care. But I made one mistake. One wrong person I aligned with. He was like a son to me. And all he did was to prove to me that my desires are indeed of greed. I lost my peace. Thanks for the help, Marina.'

Merjella patted him on his shoulders. She helped him walk towards the chopper. After a few metres, the guards took over and escorted him. The old man turned back to Merjella and informed her, 'The island now belongs to Louis. He is a good boy.'

When they reached the shore, Qwerty was already waiting. Bingo, Matio, Circa, the two Bertas, Aurelia, Zaquella, Carmello, and Mathello were in the water close to the shore, waiting to receive Merjella. Joubin was singing praises of Merjella, and everyone was in a celebratory mood.

Qwerty looked at both Ryan and Merjella quite mischievously and smiled. Merjella was holding Louis in her arms, and Ryan was standing very close to her.

'What?' questioned Merjella to Qwerty as she flew with her little wings close to her.

'Nothing.' Qwerty beamed and then asked back, 'When are you two getting married?'

They immediately realized that they were both standing too close. Ryan pulled himself a step away, complaining that she was yet to restore his sense of feel, while Merjella started to chase the teasing Qwerty, with Louis following her in that beautiful long beach.